UP TO NO GOOD

THE SIREN ISLAND SERIES, BOOK TWO

TRICIA O'MALLEY

Up To No Good
The Siren Island Series
Book Two

Cover Design:
Damonza Book Covers
Editor:
Elayne Morgan

FOR THE RESTLESS ONES — MAY YOU ALWAYS SEEK
YOUR JOY.

"Travel far enough, you meet yourself." – David Mitchell

CHAPTER 1

*L*ola didn't open her eyes as she felt the sheets move, her lover rolling from the bed. She steadied her breathing, listening as he used the bathroom and dressed quickly in the early morning light. The apartment door squeaked, hinges worn with age, the tell-tale sign that once more a man was leaving her life.

"And thank god for that," Lola said out loud, stretching decadently in the sheets that tangled around her still-naked body. Lola adhered to a strict "love 'em and leave 'em" policy that suited her lifestyle down to the bone. The few times she'd danced too closely to the flames of love, Lola had pirouetted away, with only a few singe marks on her heart.

It was better that way.

With so many men to sample, and so many places to visit, Lola approached life like the smorgasbord it was –

with gusto and great enthusiasm. So what if she rarely stayed in one country or kept a relationship for longer than a few months? If anything, it provided her with diverse life experiences and enough knowledge of men to know how to get while the getting was good.

She'd been restless of late.

Not that being restless was anything new to her – it typically signaled that it was time for her to move on.

Lola leaned across the bed and unlatched the arched window, its wood dented and splintered with age and use, and swung it open. Propping herself on the pillows, she casually rolled a cigarette – a habit she only indulged in when visiting France or Italy. Lighting it, she watched as a thin curl of smoke danced in a slim ray of sunlight. Below, a child called out in rapid Italian, his mother responding harshly, and slowly the small fishing village hugging the coast of the Mediterranean sprang to life.

There were worse ways to wake up, Lola mused. And yet, the scene had lost its charm for her. For a brief moment, Lola allowed herself to wallow in melancholy as she listened to friends and family greet each other on the narrow cobblestone street beneath the apartment.

The life she'd cultivated was a rich and fascinating one, Lola thought, as smoke curled into the air around her.

So why did she feel so empty?

CHAPTER 2

Three men gathered around a woman sipping an espresso at a miniscule bistro tucked beneath a stone archway of a bridge, a sliver of the Mediterranean just visible through the buildings that clambered on top of each other, battling to claim a piece of that million-dollar view. The woman laughed, tossing a head of startlingly white hair, and reached out to playfully swat one of her adoring suitors on the shoulder.

Lola couldn't help but smile.

"There she is! My darling!" Lola's mother, Miriam, rose and rushed forward to sweep Lola into a bone-shattering hug, though they'd just seen each other days before.

"I see you're enjoying your breakfast," Lola said, while her mother held her at arm's length and scrutinized her with a calculating look that only a mother could give.

"Always. There's nothing like a fine cup of Italian espresso in the company of adoring men. You know how I love the Italians," Miriam said, her smooth black linen shift flowing softly around her, a chunky necklace of intricate hoops taking the outfit from simple to interesting. It was something Miriam had an uncanny knack for – polishing up the mundane and making it shine – which made her a highly sought-after art curator. From hotel chains to private villas, her mother's clients paid her to travel the world and source art pieces for their spaces. The job suited Miriam's lifestyle perfectly, and Lola often found herself tagging along on a trip between her own various business ventures.

"I think all of Italy knows how much you love the Italians," Lola drawled, and Miriam laughed, unoffended.

"They do make delightful lovers, so long as you don't get attached. What's not to like? They're charming, they compliment you, and they're completely comfortable with no commitments. I adore traveling here," Miriam said, settling back into her chair, crossing her slim legs, and blowing a kiss to the men who had wandered away once she'd ignored them to focus on Lola.

It had always been this way with her mother, Lola mused with a small smile as she signaled the waitress for an espresso. Their relationship was closer to that of best friends than parent and child. She'd grown accustomed to it, and was often surprised to realize how much her friends struggled in their relationships with their parents. Miriam was… Miriam, Lola decided: effusive, affectionate, supportive, and always up for an adventure.

"I can't say I blame you," Lola agreed, stretching her legs out to admire her new sandals. Another thing to love about Italy was their handiwork with leather. "You've picked a particularly pretty part to visit this time."

"Isn't it grand?" Miriam said, sweeping her hand out at the sea. "I just love all these little villages tucked along the coast. They're all so similar and yet so wildly different. I've found some marvelous pieces for my clients already."

"It really is," Lola said. She nodded her thanks to the waitress and took her first biting sip of the espresso, the taste invigorating her.

"Darling, I must say, I just love that color on you. That deep lavender is so nice against the red in your hair right now. It pops your eyes as well, but as your mother I can't help but notice the dark circles beneath them. Were you up late? Did you meet someone?" Miriam leaned in, her face creased with concern.

"I did meet someone," Lola said, and Miriam's face lit up in interest.

"Do tell."

"He was nice." Lola waved her lover away without a second thought. "But I haven't been sleeping well recently. I'm feeling… restless, I suppose."

"Time for another trip?" Miriam asked, sliding a

slim cigarette from a gold-encrusted case and lighting it with a mother-of-pearl lighter.

"I'm on a trip now," Lola pointed out.

"True, but there's always the next adventure." Miriam shrugged. "What are you looking for?"

"Isn't that the million-dollar question? I love my life," Lola said. "I love the freedom of it and the experiences I've been able to have."

"Absolutely, darling. Just think of all the places you've been, the people you've met! I'm so happy that you've lived the life you have already. I'd never wish mediocrity on you." Miriam shuddered at the mere thought and tapped her cigarette in the ashtray.

"No, I certainly wouldn't either," Lola laughed. "I just keep thinking that I need to build something or make something of all… this." Lola spread her hands out to encompass the area around them.

"Well, you sort of are, aren't you, darling? You write your wonderful travel articles, your photos sell marvelously, and you've made connections around the world."

"It just feels very fleeting. I think I need something more concrete." Lola shrugged, unsure of what she really was trying to articulate.

Miriam regarded her in horror. "You want to settle down?"

"God, no!" They both laughed at the thought. "I just meant that I've been thinking about creating something for myself. A business. Not just freelancing."

"I'm intrigued." Miriam nodded, running a finger over a slim gold band at her wrist.

"That's as far as I've gotten. It's only been in the last few weeks that I've started thinking about more. Just wanting more... of something." Lola shrugged.

"Well, your birthday is coming up. I sometimes get a bit melancholy around my birthday," Miriam mused, her bright hazel eyes – twins to Lola's – turning to the sea for a moment. "Or maybe not melancholy. Reflective, I suppose. I hope you're not having a mid-life crisis."

"I am not mid-life, Mom." Lola rolled her eyes.

"Well, you know, the mid-thirties can be a tough time for women. Everyone is getting married and having babies; you feel time ticking away and all that. It's not unusual to step back and take stock of your direction."

"You were married and had a baby," Lola pointed out, draining the rest of her espresso and signaling for the waitress.

"Good lord, I know. What was I thinking?" Miriam mused, then shook with laughter at Lola's face.

"Not the baby; I meant your father. We were always better friends than partners. I never should have married that man."

"What about the four husbands after him?" Lola asked, raising an eyebrow at Miriam.

"Flights of fancy, dear. I can't be held accountable for my impulsive soul." Miriam shrugged, completely unapologetic that she was currently on the hunt for husband number six.

"Why marry them, though?" Lola wondered, after she ordered a pastry and another espresso from the waitress.

"Why, darling, it's just the most fun. All the pomp and circumstance! Pretty dresses and a big party? Who wouldn't love that? There's nothing wrong with celebrating love. It's the most important thing in the world, after all."

Lola wondered briefly if her mother could accurately assess the difference between lust and love, but since she herself was no expert on the matter, she decided to drop it.

"As long as you're happy, you know I'm happy," Lola said.

"And same for you, my beautiful daughter. Which is why I'm worried that you're in this funk. You know… I think I know just the thing. A colleague of mine was telling me about this psychic who lives in the village just over. I believe she reads tea leaves, or palms, or something like that. We must go. Are you busy this afternoon?"

"No, I sent my photo catalogue to the editor this morning," Lola said.

"Marvelous!" Miriam clapped her hands, delighted at the prospect of a new adventure. It was impossible not to love her mother's enthusiasm for life. "It's a date."

"To the psychic we go," Lola agreed, tapping her

espresso cup against her mother's and leaning back to watch the people of the village wander past. Life went on, one way or the other, but it was always better with an adventure on the horizon.

CHAPTER 3

"*A*re you certain you know where you're going?" Lola asked as Miriam tugged her down yet another twisty alley running through the backstreets of the neighboring village.

"Of course not," Miriam declared, a wide-brimmed hat shading the sun from her face. "That's what makes it an adventure."

Lola raised the battered Leica camera at her waist. In a movement as natural as taking her next breath, she framed a shot of an old man reading a newspaper on the stoop of a crumbling building, the bright blue of the door providing an interesting contrast to his buttoned-up shirt in muted shades of red. She supposed it didn't really matter if they got lost; she had nothing on her agenda for the foreseeable future. But there was a part of her that – every once in a while – liked to know where she was going. Perhaps that was what was currently bothering her, Lola mused as she took another picture, this time of the light filtering through the waxy leaves of a vine clinging to a wall.

"Here we are," Miriam declared, coming to a stop in front of an arched doorway. The door was painted a deep purple with a gold knocker in the shape of a gargoyle, and a faded sign with the word *Indovino* scrawled in wispy font hung above it. Lola automatically snapped a picture before her mother rapped neatly on the door with her knuckles.

"*Benvenuto*. Come." A woman, close to Miriam's age, stood in the open doorway. Lola's hands itched to take her picture as well, but she knew it would be rude to do so. A kaleidoscope of colors encircled the woman, from the scarves woven through her long hair to the tangle of necklaces dripping from her neck. Layers of fabric flowed behind her as she turned and traipsed into the dim interior of her home, apparently assuming Lola and her mother would follow.

Lola immediately liked the woman's vibe – a no-nonsense *take me or leave me* type of attitude – and followed her through a dim hallway to a cozy room where low cushioned chairs surrounded a circular table draped in silks. In one corner, an etched glass lampshade portrayed Cupid with his bow; in another a reproduction Warhol Campbell's soup can print hung in a gilded navy-blue frame. Shelves lined one wall, covered in statues of dancing pagans and bobblehead gnomes. The room should have looked cluttered, but somehow the overall effect just worked. Lola could all but see the wheels turning in Miriam's head as she looked around the room with a dreamy smile on her face.

"My name is Aurora, and I welcome you so long as you welcome me." Aurora spoke in thickly accented English, her gaze not missing a trick as she scanned their faces. Lola felt a pulse of energy push at her and automatically pushed back in her mind, a method she'd learned when she was very young to shield herself from others. If pressed to explain it, she could no more explain the mental tricks she did to protect herself and her energy than she could explain her preference for pistachio gelato over chocolate. It just was.

"Ah," Aurora said, her brown eyes narrowing as they focused on Lola. Then she beckoned them to sit as she bent and arranged her dress around her as she took her own seat by the low table.

"I'm Miriam, and this is my daughter Lola," Miriam said, sitting and smoothly crossing her legs at her ankles. "It's lovely to meet you. Thank you for welcoming us into your space."

It was something Lola had always appreciated about her mother and had learned from her. No matter how off-putting, strange, or awkward the people or situation might be, Miriam treated everyone they encountered in their travels with a graciousness and kindness that ultimately ended up earning her the respect of whomever they met.

"You are welcome here. Please, tell me, may I offer

you some tea?" Aurora asked, gesturing to a small table along the wall with a kettle and cups.

"Oh, is that what you do? Read tea leaves?" Miriam said, smiling once more.

"I do not, my lady; what I need to know comes from here." Aurora touched first her forehead, then her heart, and then the faded pack of tarot cards that sat before her on the table.

"Silly me – I wasn't entirely sure what you were offering," Miriam said.

"It is fine. Divination comes in all forms. Reading the leaves is not for me," Aurora shrugged. "How may I be of help today?"

"My daughter is feeling restless with her direction. I heard of your services from Pietro at the woodworking shop."

"Ah, yes, Pietro. Fine man," Aurora said, a whisper of a smile flowing over her face.

"He is," Miriam agreed, and both women chuckled in appreciation, making Lola want to roll her eyes and laugh at the same time. Only her mother could meet someone who had been with the same man as she, laugh in appreciation of his services, and not show a trace of jealousy.

"Shuffle the cards," Aurora said, handing the cards over to Lola. She took them, feeling their age in the worn corners and the energy that zapped through them. She shuffled, admiring the dainty faded floral design on the back of the card, wondering what it was she was here for. This certainly wasn't her first time visiting a psychic or tarot card reader – Lola embraced all kinds of divination – so she knew she needed to focus her intention on what she wanted to learn from the cards. Schooling her mind to stillness, Lola tried to let her energy flow into the cards, asking for her next direction in life.

Aurora mumbled in Italian as she took the cards back and began to flip them open on the table in an intricate design, working her way through a large portion of the deck and fanning them out in a circle.

"Oh, those are lovely," Lola gasped despite herself, and leaned forward to examine the images depicted on the cards, where mermaids cavorted with men, danced beneath the waves, or basked in the wan moonlight on dark shores.

"*Grazie*," Aurora murmured, her eyes intent on the cards as she tapped her finger on the table. Then she turned her gaze to Lola. "You are in a time of transition."

"More or less." Lola shrugged. She was always in transition, so this was nothing new to her.

"Here," Aurora said, bringing her clenched palm to her heart. "In your soul. Transitioning. Ascending."

"Is she sick?" Miriam gasped, reaching out to clench Lola's arm.

"No, in her path. What she's here to learn. Her soul is ascending. As though up a ladder to the next level, you understand?" Aurora said, tapping her finger on a card where a mermaid held a mirror to her face. "This is a time of big soul growth. Lessons to learn."

"I see," Miriam breathed, leaning over to look at the card.

"Aren't we always learning, though?" Lola asked, her eyes meeting Aurora's.

"We are. But this time period is big for you. You feel discontent. The cards say it is time for a new venture," Aurora pressed.

"An adventure!" Miriam clapped, delighted.

"A *venture*. Like a business venture," Lola clarified, and Aurora nodded her agreement.

"Well, you were just talking about that this morning, darling," Miriam said.

"I was," Lola agreed.

"What should she do?" Miriam asked, her eyes searching the cards.

"She must take all her skills, all her travels, and funnel them into one spot," Aurora said, waving her hand in a circle in the air.

"Easier said than done," Lola argued. "There isn't really a job that encompasses all of my talents."

"Isn't there?" Aurora said, pursing her lips as she studied the cards once more. "I don't believe that to be true."

"Plus, I don't want to work that hard for something I don't love," Lola said, feeling a frisson of frustration work its way through her gut. "I am more than content with the money I earn from my freelance gigs. I don't

need or want for much; I always can make money if I
need it."

"This isn't about money, but about joy," Aurora
said.

"I'm joyful," Lola burst out, but even to her it
sounded defensive.

"You see, you work for others all the time. You may
love what you do, but you would love it more if you...
how do you say? Umbrella." Aurora held up her palms
and made an arching motion over their heads, the
bracelets at her wrists tinkling. "Put it all under one
umbrella. You. You must sell you."

"I don't know that I'm that interesting of a brand,"
Lola murmured.

"You underestimate. You've learned much. Use it,"
Aurora said, her eyes back on the cards. "But the opportunity is not yet here. You must travel."

"So there *is* an adventure. Perfect. Where to?"
Miriam asked, leaning forward once more.

"*La sirena*." Aurora tapped a card and looked up,
narrowing her eyes at Lola. "This makes sense to you?"

"It does," Lola said.

"Where?" Miriam looked between them.

"There's a man," Aurora continued, ignoring Miriam's gasp of excitement.

"There's always a man," Lola said, her eyebrow
raised.

Aurora studied the cards some more before looking
back at Lola. "This one matters. Pay attention," she said.

"They all matter. Until they don't," Lola argued.

Miriam sighed. "I suspect I am guilty of teaching you that," she said, sadness etching her pretty face.

"It's not a bad thing, Mom," Lola said, turning to her mother in surprise. "You've taught me to be independent, to stand for myself, and to – no matter what – know that I can find my own happiness. That's an incredible lesson."

"But, my darling, there can be such joy to allowing a partner to share your life. I'd hate for you lose that opportunity because you're too busy moving on," Miriam said.

"Like you have?" Lola asked. The words sounded harsher than she meant them to, which was reflected in Miriam's wince.

"I will always believe in love. It may make me seem silly or flighty to the outside world, but I'm a hopeless romantic and I plan to be until the day I die," Miriam said.

Lola immediately leaned over to press a kiss to her mother's cheek. "You are perfectly imperfect, mother of mine. And I couldn't have asked for a better role model. You're right, I shouldn't close myself off to the possibility of love."

"You'll know," Aurora mused, having leaned back to watch them both. "You have the sight."

"You do?" Miriam gasped, turning to measure Lola.

"I mean… I have something," Lola admitted, shrugging it away. It wasn't something she thought of or examined too deeply.

"How have you not told me this?" Miriam demanded.

"The sight is private. You share it when you are ready." Aurora nodded her head, setting her scarves in motion.

"I guess I'd say I'm good at reading energy, I know when people are lying, and I get flashes of the future at times," Lola said.

"You can see the future?" Miriam's voice went up an octave.

"Just flashes. A gut knowledge. But it's not like divination. I wouldn't be able to say to you, 'You'll get this big promotion and move to Portugal.' It isn't until after something happens that I'll look back and realize I knew what would happen," Lola said, struggling with how to explain her gifts.

"You can train," Aurora said, sweeping the cards back into a neat pile. "You can teach yourself to become better."

"I don't know if that's what I want," Lola admitted.

"You'll know, if the time is right, when to delve deeper," Aurora said, and held out the deck of cards. "A gift."

Lola leaned back, her hands in the air, and shook her head. "I can't take your cards. These are a work of art. And the years of energy! No, please. This isn't necessary."

"I insist. They're meant for you," Aurora said, and nodded her head toward a shelf covered with boxes of tarot cards, in every material and color. "I know when a deck has chosen to move on. These are for you."

"What a splendid gift, Lola. You must take them. The artwork on the cards alone – well, you could study it for days," Miriam gushed, beaming at Aurora.

"*La sirena*. Remember her. She is here," Aurora said, touching her chest once more.

"Thank you, Aurora. You've been very kind today," Lola said, and reached out a hand. The psychic grasped hers for a moment, her gaze steady, as a warm rush of energy pulsed through Lola.

"Allow change. It's the only way you grow," Aurora murmured and released Lola's hand.

"I feel like I'm constantly changing. I'm the least routine person I know, aside from my mother," Lola said as they stood to leave.

"That *is* your normal, then, yes?"

CHAPTER 4

*T*he plane, a little twelve-seater, dipped on a gust of wind as it banked right and circled over the island. Lola, still groggy from a day of travel, blinked her eyes as they cut through a single chunky cloud and sun exploded onto the turquoise water below.

Siren Island beckoned, as it had since the day Lola had stumbled on a travel blogger's posts about the sleepy island in the Caribbean, and she'd known – deep within – that something awaited her here. Perhaps it was why she'd all but shoved her friend, Sam, onto a plane headed for this island when she'd recently had a melt-down after a particularly bad time in her career. Now Sam was living here fulltime, and Lola couldn't ignore the call of the island. On the face of things, she was visiting to check on her friend and meet her new man, but Lola knew there was more. *La sirena*, the psychic had murmured, and Lola had known it was time. Time to visit Siren Island, time for a reassessment of her life, time for whatever waited for her here to come to fruition.

Granted, she probably should have checked if Sam was going to be on-island before she'd impulsively booked her flights, but by the time she'd reached her friend, Lola was already on her way to Amsterdam for her connecting flight. Luckily, Samantha would be heading back to Siren Island shortly. In the meantime, Lola had booked a room at the Laughing Mermaid B&B – the same place she had pushed Sam into booking a room at not so long ago. Perhaps it was the name, or the gut feeling, but Lola had known it would be just the medicine her best friend needed.

And now, as the plane bounced lightly on the single lane tarmac, she wondered if it would be the same for her – if that which called to her had the power to save her.

"Welcome to Siren Island." The flight attendant continued with his welcome speech, but it was lost on Lola as she turned the name over in her head. Siren Island. The Sirens had always been a particular point of interest for both her and Miriam, and they often sourced pieces of art that depicted mermaids and the like from around the world for clients. There was an endless fasci-nation with these beings of the deep – ones who lived life on their terms – and Lola was hypnotized by their myths, as was much of the rest of the world. A little buzz of excitement hummed through her as she ducked through the small door and clambered down the steps leading to the tarmac to wait in the sun by the side of the plane as they unloaded the few pieces of luggage.

Lola typically traveled with a leather backpack, the contents of which she'd honed to create as easy a travel experience as possible. She carried few clothes, all brightly patterned or plain black to hide dirt; one swimsuit; a pashmina that could double as a blanket or a beach cover-up; two pairs of shoes; one hat; and a canvas jacket. Her laptop and notebooks went into the tote that she carried with her. She liked to pick up extra accessories and items when she traveled if she needed to add more spice to her outfits. One thing Lola had quickly learned as she'd wandered the world was that you could wear the same outfit several days in a row without most people paying much attention, and switching up a scarf or jewelry could quickly update an outfit. She laughed a little as she thought back to her first years traveling around the world and all the luggage she'd lugged around – for what? Nothing but headaches and bags lost on their way to Tokyo.

Lola smiled her thanks at the baggage porter and swung the backpack over her shoulders, tucking her burnished amber braid back and sliding silver aviators onto her face to block the unrelenting sun. Following the small line of people, she breezed her way through customs where an agent flirted with her, offering to give her his own private tour of the island. Lola politely declined.

It wasn't uncommon for men to flirt with her. With her tumbling hair, generous curves that had embarrassed her when she was younger, and a mile-wide smile, Lola seemed to appeal to the baser needs of men. She supposed it didn't hurt that once she'd discovered the joys of sex and the companionship of men, Lola had embraced a more worldly approach to taking lovers. She'd always enjoyed men and was of the opinion they were to be sampled – much like canapes from a passing appetizer plate at a party.

Speaking of appetizers... Lola's attention was caught by a man striding across the parking lot of the small airport. Wasn't he delicious, Lola thought as she studied him from behind the cool shade of her sunglasses. Gilded hair tumbled out of a small leather cord tied at the nape of his neck. A faded linen shirt, sleeves rolled – and buttons opened lower than necessary in Lola's opinion – revealed a deeply tanned chest where several necklaces tangled together. Fitted army-green pants covered muscular legs. The man waved a hand, shouting something to someone across the parking lot, and throwing his head back to laugh when the man responded. Ignoring the punch in her gut at his inarguable appeal, Lola rolled her eyes lightly behind her glasses.

She knew his type: faintly European, somewhat exotic, well aware of his manliness, and likely to have throngs of gaggling women – usually twenty years younger – hovering around him. Her suspicions were immediately confirmed when he greeted a group of women who had, moments before, been standing around arguing with each other. When their eyes landed on the Adonis walking their way, every woman in the group had immediately straightened and checked her hair. In moments, he had the group laughing and simpering around him.

Lola shook her head as she moved toward the taxi stand. But even she wasn't entirely immune to the man's appeal, and she glanced at him once more – to find him staring at her. Holding his look, Lola was surprised to see his mouth tighten for a moment before he gave her a subtle nod. Lola returned it, refusing to smile – refusing to acknowledge the age-old awareness that ran straight through her, screaming that this man would be a part of her life.

"Lola?"

Lola turned, blocking from her mind the images of her tumbling into bed with the golden man, and smiled at the woman who approached her. With salt and pepper hair falling almost to her waist, an easy flowing dress in the colors of sunset, and a smile that lit her face, Lola knew this had to be the owner of the Laughing Mermaid B&B, whom Sam held in such high regard.

"Irma?"

"Yes, welcome," Irma said, folding Lola into a hug.

Her touch was warm and welcoming, and Lola instantly knew two things.

She was home.

And the woman who hugged her was not entirely of this world.

CHAPTER 5

This was one of those times that Lola wished her extrasensory sight was stronger than it was. She was dying to know more about Irma. Energy seemed to crackle around her like a live wire. Lola was surprised Samantha hadn't mentioned the sheer impact of this woman. That being said, Samantha didn't read people the same way Lola did. God love her, but Sam was as different from Lola as a cheetah from a tortoise.

"I'm delighted to finally meet you," Irma said, gently tugging Lola's bag from her shoulder and putting it in the bed of a dusty pickup truck. "Samantha has told us so much about you."

"I hope all good," Lola said automatically, unable to stop her gaze from sliding out the window to look for the sexy man in the parking lot. "I don't always have the best reputation."

"Those *are* the best reputations, to my mind at least." Irma chuckled as she shifted into first and headed toward the edge of the small airport parking lot. "You're not living life right if there aren't at least a few people talking about you."

"I like that," Lola laughed. "It's a more positive way of looking at being judged."

"People just judge what they fear," Irma said, her eyes following Lola's. "Handsome, isn't he?"

"Who? Oh," Lola said, openly ogling the man at this point, "handsome and knows it, I'd say."

"I like a man with confidence." Irma followed the slow-moving line of cars exiting the airport.

"That's the truth of it, isn't it? We want our men with backbones, and then get annoyed when they stand up to us," Lola nodded, her grin widening as the man turned and met her smile through the window. Even from here, she could feel the pull of him, and his long slow smile only served to let her know he was nothing but trouble.

"Gage isn't a doormat, that's for certain." Irma laughed again and waved, shaking her finger lightly in Gage's direction, and he blew a kiss. "He knows what he's about. Don't mind him. For the most part, he's harmless, though I don't think you're the type to have any trouble handling men."

"No, I most certainly don't." Lola watched as the group of women swarmed Gage once more. She deliberately turned her head away from the sight, batting down the feeling of annoyance that threatened her. What did she care if this man was a flirt? For god's sake, she didn't even know him. "Though I love a holiday romance as much as the next person, I'm not particularly interested in a dalliance this vacation. I've other things on my mind to sort out."

"Well, I'd never let the sorting out of life get in the way of a dalliance, but that's just me," Irma laughed. "You could do worse than Gage."

"I likely have done worse than Gage," Lola agreed. "But that's neither here nor there. I'm just looking forward to seeing what I hear is your gorgeous villa and relaxing." The Gages of the world would just have to wait.

"Your wish is my command," Irma said, pulling into the street. She kept up a stream of chatter as they wound their way through a tiny downtown and up a road that eventually turned into a dirt road before Irma turned at a small mermaid statue tucked at the base of a tree. With virtually no other indication or sign that there was a street, Lola was certain she would have missed the turn if she'd been tasked with finding the B&B from the airport on her own.

"I like the vibe of this island," Lola commented, biting her tongue to keep from asking more about the particular vibe that Irma gave off. "It's not overly developed, and it seems... real, somehow. Not like some fake tourist destination where everything is shiny and perfect. I like places that feel authentic."

"That's kind of you," Irma said, pulling to a stop in front of a pretty white-washed villa tucked among the shade of several large palm trees. "I'm particularly fond of this island, myself. I've been here my whole life. I couldn't leave it if I tried."

The words were true, Lola could read that instantly, but they were true in a way that didn't make sense to her – as if Irma meant them literally. She wanted to more closely examine the feeling that pressed at her, but Irma was already popping out of the truck and slinging Lola's satchel over her shoulder.

"I can get that," Lola said. However, Irma was striding through an arched doorway and up a winding staircase. Lola followed, tucking her tote over her shoulder, wanting to stop and examine the beautiful paintings that lined the staircase.

"Welcome to the Soul Voyage room," Irma said, pushing open a heavy wooden door, her face creasing in a smile.

"That's a unique name," Lola said, stopping just steps inside the room to let out a little sigh of delight. "And this is a perfect room for it. Irma, you've outdone yourself here."

"I have to give credit to my daughters on this one. Jolie and Mirra had their way with it."

"They can have their way with my place, the next time I own one, if this is the result."

A circular bed dominated the room. It was ringed in a canopy of thin, wispy, white netting and twinkle lights, creating an otherworldly effect that reminded Lola of stars peeking through a cloud. The ceiling was painted a deep navy, the walls a crisp white, and her eyes were drawn to a brilliant tapestry rug in rich golden hues, the color of a sunset. As Lola looked around the room, she realized that the girls had created a journey, from the sunset to the dark night on the ceiling, with the twinkle lights of stars and ethereal clouds in between. Along the long wall behind the bed was a narrow photograph that showcased the perfect turquoise blue of the ocean's edge meeting the sand.

"It's the world," Lola breathed.

"Or their interpretation of it," Irma agreed.

"It's cleverly done," Lola said, turning to scan the room, her eyes landing on the beautiful French doors, draped in white linen curtains matching the ones on the bed, the ocean a stunning backdrop. Lola imagined she could lie in bed and watch the sun set over the water. "Too often I see people try to pull off an idea in such a literal manner that it becomes trite or overdone. This is fantastic."

"Thank you," Irma beamed, crossing her arms across her chest and leaning against the doorframe.

"I've had a good feeling about your place ever since I discovered it online, and I was even more sold on it after Samantha had such a great experience here. But now? I can see this is going to be a wonderful stay."

"We'll do our best to make it so," Irma said. "Come down to the garden if you'd like. We'll be having a drink for sunset. Otherwise, if you're ready to crash out after a long day of travel, you'll find some snacks in the fridge in your kitchenette and we'll see you tomorrow."

"Thank you, Irma. Truly, I think this is going to be exactly what I need right now."

"One can only hope," Irma said with an enigmatic smile as she closed the door, leaving Lola to look out at the water and dream.

Lola had stayed in a myriad of places throughout her travels, from yurts to five-star resorts, yet she found herself uniquely charmed by the room. It hit the right notes of comfort and imagination, seeming to invite her to kick her feet up and dream of 'what may come' while the waves crashed outside her window.

Digging through her leather backpack, Lola quickly changed her clothes. She wrapped a sarong around her body, knotting it in a twist around her neck to form a loose island-style dress. Humming, she took some time to put her things away, settling into the room, then heated water for a cup of tea. When her hands brushed the mermaid tarot cards in her pack, Lola pulled out the gilded box and wandered to her balcony, her tea cooling on the table next to a low-slung chair of braided rope.

There hadn't been much time to assess what the psychic had said to her in Italy, as – in typical Lola fashion – she'd booked flights and left the country the following day. Miriam had already been on her way to

Croatia for an art exhibition. Now that the flurry of travel had passed, Lola settled into the chair, charmed to discover that she could swing in it, and opened the box of cards.

"Hmm, these really are works of art," Lola said, crossing her legs in the chair and using her toe to set it moving. She gently thumbed through the cards, weathered with use and age, and let the flow of energy fill her.

Lola hadn't always known she was different. It wasn't until high school, when her gut instincts had proven correct about a thief in their classroom, that she had realized not everyone felt the pulses of mental energy like she did. The ability to read energy, see auras, or get a flash of insight into the future had guided her path in life; the few times she hadn't listened to herself, instead following what others thought best for her, had ended horribly.

Like the time she'd tried to work in accounting. Lola chuckled as she drew out another mermaid card and studied it. She'd been wildly unsuited for the job, something Sam had delicately tried to point out, yet Lola had wanted to give a normal nine-to-five job a go. She had considered it an experiment, she supposed, wanting to see what all the fuss about the dream of a corporate job, two-point-five kids, and a white picket fence was all about. It hadn't ended well, to say the least. She had dealt with a furious boss who questioned her knowledge of spreadsheets, and weathered a bone-deep sadness from following the same routine every day – essentially staring at the four grey walls of her cubicle, the fluorescent lighting turning her skin a sallow sickly color.

Lola had up and quit within four months, much to the relief of her coworkers and friends. She'd eventually realized that her co-workers were happy to see her go not only because of the mistakes she was making at work, but because she asked so many questions, with genuine interest, about why anyone would submit themselves to this on a daily basis when there was so much of the world to explore. It wasn't likely they enjoyed being reminded of the dullness of their existence, and they'd eyed Lola as if she was a glittery nymph who had bounced her way into the office, having gotten lost on the way to ice dancing lessons.

It had taken her a few years to understand that everyone's dreams were different – for some, routine was a balm to their soul, while others, like herself, craved constant change. She'd also grown comfortable with being judged, knowing that not everyone was capable of understanding the life she chose to live, and instead contented herself with feeding her soul from her travels and her artistic pursuits. For the most part, Lola *was* happy.

There was just a niggling "but" that was making Lola probe deeper. That was something she didn't shy away from doing, as she felt it was vitally important to be in touch with her feelings, not only in order to trust her extrasensory sight, but also to create art. Unfortunately, feelings weren't always the comfortable and fun ones like joyfulness and play, and Lola knew she'd be doing herself a disservice if she ignored the yucky emotions only to focus on the good ones. The uncomfortable bit was where growth happened, Lola reminded herself, and the psychic had told her she was at a time of great soul growth.

"Okay, my beauties," Lola said, shuffling the tarot cards in her hand. "What do I need to focus on while I'm here?"

She pulled out a card of a mermaid looking in the mirror – the same one the psychic had pulled in Italy – and nodded. It was a card about self-examination, taking the time to see who she really was, and knowing herself through and through. Which often meant embracing her faults, which was not fun to do. Maybe on this trip she'd need to learn to find a way to celebrate her faults and use them to her advantage, instead of considering them weaknesses. Pulling out a notebook, she jotted a note down about perhaps doing a photo study around the island where perceived weaknesses were actually strengths.

Idly, she pulled another card. This one showcased a man cradling a mermaid, her hair tumbling down over her shoulder, in complete submission to him. Vulnerability. It was something Miriam embraced easily, opening her heart repeatedly with enthusiasm, always willing to fall in love. Lola struggled with being vulnerable; she preferred to rely upon herself and nobody else, and it was a trait she would definitely consider more of a fault than a strength.

She placed the two cards next to each other, and stared out to sea.

CHAPTER 6

*L*ola was up early the next morning, having enjoyed a relaxing evening to herself on her balcony, sipping tea and sketching beach scenes. Her eyes had been drawn to two curvy beauties on the beach, who she could only assume were the infamous Jolie and Mirra. She'd smirked to herself, knowing how discomfiting they must have been to the tidy Samantha, and hoped to chat with the women soon. If anything, she'd beg them to let her draw or photograph them – in fact, all of the women at the Laughing Mermaid B&B were a study in edges and softness. Lola itched to shoot their portraits in stark black and white.

Donning flowy harem pants in a mosaic red, teal, and orange print, along with a snug black tank, Lola braided her hair loosely and slung her leather satchel over her shoulder, her trusty Leica hanging around her neck. She slipped from the room and strode down the stairs, more than ready to explore the island. Her time spent sketching last night had led to vivid dreams which in turn had left her burning to do something creative this morning. The best way for her to work through this emotion was to get out and explore the island, letting it show her its secrets.

With no direction in mind, Lola began to walk down the dirt road, smiling as an iguana skittered past her feet, and enjoying the light breeze that cooled the morning air. Pausing, she stopped to take a photo of a succulent that had grown through a hole in a craggy volcanic rock, and she enjoyed the juxtaposition of the soft green petals against the sharp edges of the rock.

Hearing a truck rumbling along, Lola stuck out her thumb automatically. She had comfortably hitchhiked all over the world. For the most part, Lola operated on the belief that people were genuinely good. She'd yet to run into problems traveling alone, and if someone gave her a bad vibe on her internal radar, she removed herself from the situation.

"Need a ride?"

Lola's head came up, like a lioness sniffing a threat in the air. But this wasn't a threat to her body – oh no, it was to her equilibrium and her emotional well-being. She scanned Gage, who looked every inch a rugged delicious specimen of a man, and reminded herself what this trip was about – though her lusty side begged her to accept a very different kind of ride from him.

"I wouldn't say I need a ride, no; I'm more than

content to walk. But I'll hop in if you're heading toward town."

"Do you often get in cars with strange men?" Gage asked, his tone placid as he watched her clamber into the vehicle, her camera bouncing off her chest.

"No, just you. Most of the men are much more normal," Lola said, unable to resist baiting him. When his grin flashed white in his tanned face, Lola considered it a win.

"Touché," Gage said, shifting the truck into gear. They motored on, the car and the man and the hum of sexual energy he gave off creating a nearly irresistible environment for Lola. There were just some men, and Gage was certainly one of them, who were completely confident in their masculinity, their sexuality, and their place in the world. It was like this cloak of raw power hung over him, and Lola found herself crossing her legs and trying not to fidget. She imagined Gage was like catnip for all the ladies out there. If she was honest with herself, she wouldn't mind rolling around with him either.

"Where are you headed today?"

Lola tuned back in from her thoughts and glanced at Gage, his eyes hidden behind mirrored aviators, his hair pulled back in the leather strap again.

"I have no plans. Wherever you'd like to drop me is fine. I want to wander about, get my bearings, maybe rent a scooter or a bicycle at some point. For now, I'd just like to take a look at what this beautiful island has to offer."

"I'll be stopping by the marina to get my boat ready for the day. It's not far from town, so that should be a central enough point for you to walk around," Gage said.

"Perfect, thank you," Lola said, twisting her braid around her finger as she deliberately stared out the window, though she was dying to pick up her camera and take a picture of Gage. She'd title it "Sure Thing."

"How long –"

"So you're staying with Irma?"

They both spoke at once, and Lola grinned, shifting to look at him as he drove.

"Yes, I'm at their guesthouse. She's lovely and the room is fantastic. I like the creative energy they've poured into it."

"They do a good business."

"I haven't met everyone there yet – I stayed in my room last night to recharge my batteries and spend some time figuring out my next project."

"Is this a project for work then? Or are you an artist?" Gage turned off the dirt road onto a more main road. That wasn't saying much – it was still basically one lane, but this section was covered in cracked pavement, smattered with hastily-patched potholes. A few palm trees dotted the road, and in the distance, Lola could see the brightly colored buildings of town.

"Both. All and the same. Work, yes, if the project

turns into something I want to sell, but sometimes I take joy in creating and not selling. I'm sort of a jack of all trades, I suppose," Lola said, not wanting to give him much more. Typically, she was an open book about her life, as her enthusiasm about all things creative and beautiful in the world bubbled out of her. But for some reason, this man had her putting walls up. She wasn't sure of her thoughts on him, his energy, and what her niggling sixth sense was saying – that he would be in her life. For that reason alone, she preferred being more reticent about the finer details of her life.

"And? What's the project?" Gage asked, slanting a look at her before returning his eyes to the road.

"Me," Lola blurted, before immediately reminding herself that she wanted to keep her walls up with him.

"Ah, a light undertaking then," Gage said, a small smile tugging at his lips.

"Right? I'm sure I'll have it all figured out by the end of the day." Despite herself, Lola let out a bold laugh, and was intrigued when she caught Gage's hands tightening on the wheel.

"That's quite a laugh you have," Gage said, surprising Lola with his forwardness.

"So I've been told."

"It makes me think of long lustful nights and cool island mornings," Gage said, pulling his truck into a space by the marina. A multitude of boats were tied to their moorings, deckhands polishing hulls or carrying supplies across the long planked docks.

Heat spiked low in Lola's gut, and she turned to meet what she could only imagine was Gage's assessing look behind his mirrored glasses.

"Something I'm sure you have a lot of experience with," Lola said, allowing an edge to creep into her voice as she nodded toward the gaggle of women simpering by the dock. "Your fan club, I presume?"

"Yes." Gage's smile spread wide in his face, and damn if it didn't make Lola want to smile right back. "Care to join?"

"I'm all good," Lola said, turning to open her car door. "I don't like joining clubs. I tend to be a loner by nature."

"That can get lonely."

"Not if you're doing it right," Lola said, and then paused after she slid from the seat, fairness forcing her to not be bitchy about all the women waiting for him. Just as she didn't particularly enjoy people judging her for her love life, it wouldn't be fair to do so to him. "But enjoy yourself. Those lustful island nights are more fun if you have a partner." Lola smiled toward the tittering group of women.

"Depends on the partner," Gage said.

"That's the truth of it." Lola laughed again, and hauled her bag over her shoulder. "Thanks for the ride. I'm sure I'll see you around."

"Lola…"

"Yes?" Lola turned, her stomach flipping a little.

"Good luck on your project. Let me know if I can help."

"Ahh." Lola smiled. "This project is something I have to do on my own."

"The offer stands. Or I'd be happy to show you around the island, if you'd like to explore more than on foot."

It would be so easy to take him up on the offer, and to fall into another whirlwind casual vacation fling. But something about this man gave her the distinct feeling that he didn't do whirlwind. She suspected he'd be slow, deliberate, and keep her as long as he liked. Which, while intriguing, was not what this trip was for.

"Noted. I'll find you if I change my mind," Lola said and waved at him as she sauntered away, laughing and shaking her head a bit as the women all but squealed in delight when he left his truck.

Nope, definitely not a man she'd need to be messing with if she wanted to get her head clear on things. Feeling smug, like she was on a diet and had chosen a salad instead of cake, Lola put an extra swing in her hips just in case he was looking.

Some habits were hard to break.

CHAPTER 7

*age watched Lola leave, noting the smooth movement of her rounded hips under the brightly colored flowy pants she wore. He liked the ease with which she carried herself, her hand automatically cradling the Leica camera strung on a colorful strap around her neck, her curly hair threatening to break loose from the braid she'd woven it into. He'd be lying if he said he wasn't interested – very interested. It wasn't often a woman of her caliber crossed his path. And a lot of women did their best to do so.

Gage smiled at the group of women who surrounded him, easing expertly into his carefully curated pitch and tour explanation, as comfortable in his job as he was in his own skin. He barely noticed the women flirting with him, as they all did. It wasn't ego that made him think this; it was more the fact that he had been told he was handsome on more than one occasion, he worked in a "cool" job on a "cool" island, and women were drawn to that like bees to flowers.

Gage didn't flatter himself to think that it was just him that was the appeal. It was the package deal. There was something about the exotic nature of his job, the island locale – when combined with his looks, that made what he assumed were fairly normal women back in the real world go googly-eyed and throw themselves at him. It was part of the job, and a part that Gage didn't particularly mind, but in this moment, he wanted nothing more than to bypass the group of paisley-clad women from Kansas and follow Lola to see what kind of adventure she was getting into today. Instead he turned, to smile at the women – a sixtieth birthday party – and began answering their questions.

He loved his job, or he wouldn't be here doing it, but he also didn't need to be doing this for a living. When he'd first sailed his way to Siren Island, it had been with little direction other than where the wind took him. He'd spent years as in-house counsel for a large international production company, and had even helped in several productions – enough of them that the royalties from the movies alone were more than enough to sustain his livelihood, even without all the money he'd saved and invested while working eighty-plus hours a week. The burnout had been expected – nobody was immune to it – but he hadn't quite expected it to take the form it had.

He'd been taking a late lunch on a pretty sunny day

in Fort Lauderdale. Antsy, he'd walked the harbor aimlessly, his mind crammed full of to-do lists, as well as a particularly thorny rights case that had been thrown on top of his caseload the night before. Walking, he let his mind go, working through the problem as best he could. It was something he did often, leaving the confines of wherever he was working to stroll and let his brain figure out solutions. This time, however, his brain was refusing to address the case and kept seeming to pull his eyes toward a boatyard where several boats were listed for sale. Curious, he'd crossed the busy street to stand at the gate and peer through at the boats locked inside.

"Can I help you?" A man, his skin ruddy with wind and sun, wiped oil from his hands with a rag and ambled over to the gate.

"I... I'm not sure. I guess I was just looking at these boats for sale."

"Do you sail?"

"Nope," Gage said, smiling at the man.

"Captain?"

"Nope."

"Drive a pontoon? Jet ski? Zodiac?"

"A few of those. What do I need to know?" Gage asked, rocking back on his heels.

"All the things, my friend. You seriously want to buy a boat?"

"No clue. But, while this may be me having a mid-life crisis, I'm going to go ahead and say yes." The man laughed at Gage's cheeky smile, and unlocked the gate, ushering him in.

"Well, let's have a look then. I'll show you a few options, and then get you signed up for a few courses before you even think about sinking your money into a boat."

"You think classes first? What if I want to be impulsive here?" Gage stopped, turning to meet the man's eyes.

"You know what they say about boat ownership? There are two best days: the day you buy a boat, and the day you sell it. My goal is to make people hold onto the feeling they get when they buy the boat. It would be remiss of me to sell you something that you have no idea how to operate. If I do that, you'll fall out of love too quickly."

"That's fair. The name's Gage, by the way," Gage said, offering his hand.

"Call me Mack. I'll help you on your journey," Mack said, and so it had begun.

At the time, he'd never thought he'd leave it all and move to an island. And yet, here he was. Running tours on his gorgeous boat in his free time, overseeing a few other investments and tour operations he had on the island, and generally living life exactly as he pleased. With few commitments.

His eyes were drawn once more to the road, but Lola was long gone.

CHAPTER 8

*L*ola quickly forgot about Gage, her mind full of creative energy, and she let herself become immersed in the island. Sticking to her plan to find spots where the broken was made beautiful, she crouched to shoot a pile of shattered shells by the water, which to her looked like a mosaic piece. She could almost see the bits of shells pressed into a table top, creating their own intricate pattern, and wondered if it was something she would want to do. Considering it briefly, she shoved it aside. The last thing she needed was more projects that she couldn't finish at the moment.

Wandering, Lola followed the harbor beach walk, a pretty brick path with the brilliant blue water on one side, the road on the other, and then rows of houses and apartment buildings that led to the small downtown shopping area. With no agenda in mind, Lola drifted along, snapping shots of a tree covered in errant shoes and flip-flops, their partners missing. She idly titled the shot "Sole Tree" in her head. She had a habit of doing that – titling her pictures as though she was showing them at a gallery – and that was how her mini-exhibitions often formed.

As she walked, Lola nodded to passersby, most of who readily smiled at her as she went past. She stopped to take a shot of a mermaid statue tucked among the walls of a rock garden surrounding a bright yellow fisherman's hut.

"Mermaids are real, you know."

Lola turned to see a man, seventy years old at the very least, a shock of white closely-cropped hair framing his deep brown skin and a smiling face. She smiled at him where he sat, his bare feet extended in front of him as he casually cleaned a large silver fish.

"Is that so?"

"That's exactly so, pretty lady. You think I'd lie to you?"

"Of course not. I think we all believe in different things," Lola said, holding up her camera at him. "Mind if I take your picture?"

"I'm made for the camera, beautiful." The man shot her a cheeky grin, two of his front teeth missing, as he boomed a laugh.

"That you are," Lola agreed, crossing her arms on the garden wall. "Have you seen a mermaid?"

"Of course I've seen a mermaid." The man's mouth

dropped open and he looked around as if he could find a friend to say, *Can you believe this woman?* "They're here. I tell you that."

"Are they far out on the water? Do you see them when you fish?" Lola asked, enjoying the man's story. She wondered if his eyesight was bad – maybe he was merely seeing dolphins flitting by in the water.

"I seen them far out. I seen them close. They're where they want to be, pretty lady, that's the real matter of it all. They around for sure. It's not named Siren Island for nothing."

"Have they spoken to you?"

"Nah, they got nothing to say to an old man like me. I hear them sing, sometimes, early in the morning, greeting the sun as it rises for the day. It's..." The man brought a fist to his chest, punching his heart. "You feel it. Right here, you get me? It's like nothing else you ever heard."

"What do they look like?"

"You gon' tell me you never seen what a mermaid looks like? They're curves, you know?" The man held his hands up and made an hourglass motion with his hands. "Lush. Real women. Well, fish women. But you know. None of that skin and bones crap. You could get there, you put a bit more weight on."

"Well, that's refreshing to hear," Lola laughed.

"I mean, I'm sure you look just fine in a bikini, mind you, I'm just saying. Need some island cooking to thicken you up a bit, and then you'll be just like the mermaids."

"I'll keep that in mind," Lola said. "How often do you see them?"

"Ahh, not as much as I used to. Maybe a few times a year? It's a rare treat, and I'm not the only one, you know. There's a museum downtown with more information. You can read all the history and the myths. But let me tell you, as a man of the sea. We know. *All* the fishermen know. You're all alone out in your boat, way off shore? Yeah, they come to you. It's a gift, that it is. One the fisherman don't take for granted."

"You've never spoken with one, though?"

"Pssssh, I should be so lucky! I wish. I'm always trying to call them over. I did get a comb though. You know, in their hair? A shell comb. That was a real treat."

"Is that so? I'd love to see it," Lola said, her interest piqued.

"It's right there. My hands all bloody, but you can look at it." The man held up his hands full of fish innards, and Lola nodded, turning to look at the little stone garden table that held a bowl of shells and sea glass. Nestled in the top was what she'd initially thought to be just another shell.

"May I?" Lola asked, gesturing to the gate door.

"Of course." The man smiled at her.

"I'm Lola, by the way."

"They call me Prince." Prince puffed out his chest and laughed that booming laugh at her as he went back to cleaning his fish. Lola bent over the dish and picked up the smooth white shell, which upon closer inspection revealed tines of a comb cut into it. The minute she touched it, her heartrate sped up.

This was the real deal.

A raw current of energy pulsed from the comb, washing over her, and Lola felt almost compelled to tuck the shell into her hair and dive into the ocean. She'd never wanted to feel water around her so much as she did in this moment, and everything around her seemed to fade away until all she could hear, as if it were on loudspeaker, was the lapping of the waves against the shore. Taking a deep breath, she smelled the air, heavy with salt from the sea, and her entire being craved the caress of cool water on her skin. Closing her eyes, she breathed once more before returning the comb to the bowl, the garden around her snapping back into focus.

"You felt it then," Prince said, his eyes on hers.

"Ahhh," Lola said, blinking a bit at the rush of power she'd felt wash over her. "I suppose I did."

"Not everyone does, you know," Prince said, humming a bit as he casually flipped another fish over, making a long slice in the skin.

"It… what is that? Do you feel it?"

"I ask everybody. Nobody has the same answer. I suspect it just calls to people as needed. Or I'm thinking those who do feel it, feel it in a way that's only meant for them."

"What does it do for you?"

"For me, it brings me to laughter, childhood – a simpler time."

"Much simpler than this?" Lola asked, gesturing to where he cleaned his fish.

"Sure. No businesses to run. No food to put on the table. I love fishing, but it's for my family. It's in my blood. Passed down over generations. But times change. Life on an island gets more costly. Keeping up can be tough for some people here. So, for me, the comb takes me to simple pleasures. Laughter. Rocking in the hammock. Racing through a garden."

"Fascinating," Lola murmured, running her hand over the comb to feel the pulse of power once more. She wished she could take it with her, study it in silence in her room, and delve deeper into what she needed to learn from it.

"What it do for you? You felt something, that's for sure. You didn't even hear me when I was speaking at you."

"The ocean. Everything faded away, except for a deep craving to be cocooned in the water."

"You're mermaid then." Prince said it so easily that Lola almost choked a laugh out.

"Erm, I feel like I'd know if I was."

"It's in the blood. Most people don't feel that from the comb. You're meant for the water. You'll see. Take your time here. Look for the mermaids. They're all over the island. You'll see what you're meant to see."

"Thank you for sharing this with me, Prince. It's an honor," Lola said, smiling down at him.

"Come back and visit me, pretty lady. I'm here most days after I get in."

"I will. Next time I'll buy a fish from you if you'll sell me one."

"I'll sure do that," Prince said, whistling a tune as Lola let herself out of the gate. It wasn't until she was far down the road that she realized he had been whistling "Under the Sea" from the movie *The Little Mermaid.*

Lola laughed, her eyes drawn once again to the ocean, and she wondered… *What if?*

CHAPTER 9

*L*ola found herself in front of the dusty little museum – nothing more than a one-room hut, painted a vibrant shade of pink with faded green shutters – and she eased the door open, stepped inside, and pushed her sunglasses up on her head.

"Welcome." A woman in a tidy skirt, layers of beaded necklaces competing for attention, rose from where she sat behind a neat laptop at a small desk in the corner. "Are you visiting?"

"I am. I was directed this way by Prince," Lola said with a smile.

"That's nice of him. We always welcome visitors who actually like to learn about the history of our island. Feel free to wander around." The woman gestured to the room as though it would take Lola ages to walk through.

"Is there a fee?"

"No. But we have a donation box on that wall if

you'd like to contribute." The woman returned to her
desk. "If you have any questions, I'm happy to help,
otherwise please take your time."

"Thank you, I'll be sure to do that," Lola said, her
eyes already drawn to a mermaid painting in the corner.
The rich hues of the ocean beckoned to her. Next to it, a
large placard outlined what was titled "The Myth of
Siren Island."

Intrigued, Lola lost herself in the story of a young
fisherman named Nalachi, who quickly fell in love with a
mysterious woman who only seemed to materialize
around the full moon. So in love was he that he was
determined to find out her secret. After one particularly
passionate evening, he kept her captive – only to discover
when the sun rose that she was dying. Luckily, Nalachi
quickly brought the woman, Irmine, back to the sea,
where she changed from human to mermaid in front of
him. Desperate for Nalachi to keep her secret, Irmine
promised him her love and in return, he pledged his own.
The months that followed were sorrowful ones, as
Nalachi was pulled to other islands to start trade routes,
and he missed the full moon with Irmine. She wasn't able
to share her news with him and, distraught, she birthed
their twin daughters at sea. Nalachi finally returned at a
full moon, so determined to find Irmine that he ignored
an impending storm and took his boat out to sea, where it
shattered on a reef. With his last breaths, he sang Irmine's
song, the one she'd given to him. She found him, too far
gone for her magick to work, but in their last moments

together he met his daughters and Irmine knew he'd loved her all along. Taking his soul as hers, she placed it in a pearl around her neck and vowed to sing whenever the storms came, to alert sailors to the treacherous rocks.

Lola sighed, her heart sad for the love that had been lost between the two, and wondered if she would ever love someone that way.

"THEY SAY SHE SINGS… particularly during storms, to keep the sailors away from the reefs," the woman said.

Lola turned, surprised to find she needed to wipe her eyes. "It's a lovely story, romantic and tragic at the same time," she said.

"Do you want to hear the song?"

"You know it?"

"That I do." The woman, her brown eyes shining, opened her mouth and sang in a surprisingly sweet soprano.

Where the starlight kisses the sea, is where you'll find me. It won't be so long, for in your heart is my song.

"It's a lovely melody," Lola breathed, tugging at her camera strap. "Haunting, even."

"It really is. You'll hear wisps of the melody woven into our songs around the island. It's not our anthem, but it's there, tangled amidst all our other history."

"And they say she's still here? The same mermaid?

Do they age? I don't know enough about their mythology, I suppose," Lola said, turning back to run her eyes over the painting.

"From my understanding, they do age, but not in the same way humans do. Maybe one century of their life equals a decade of ours, or something of that nature. It's a little hard to pin down, as I'm sure you'd understand." The woman chuckled, and then excused herself to answer a phone that buzzed on her desk.

Lola moved on to the next display, which documented sightings from fishermen, as well as various myths about mermaids held the world over. In the case next to it were a few mermaid artifacts. Lola stared into the glass box, wondering how a museum could claim something as an artifact when the beings behind said artifacts weren't actually real. There was the usual array of shells, a few necklaces, several combs – but it wasn't until Lola's eyes landed on a mirror that she felt anything.

The rest... well, she could dismiss those as pretty shells or small art pieces. But the mirror – someone had gotten that right. It seemed almost to glow with energy. The mirror was slightly chipped, lined in gold with a lovely dusky pink pearl background. Whatever this mirror was or wherever it came from, it had power. Lola closed her eyes and went inside herself for a moment – she needed to know if it was a bad energy. All she felt, though, was a gentle wash of love and approval, as though the mirror only asked for her to look inside and love what she saw.

Lola opened her eyes, almost snorting. Wasn't that exactly what she was on this trip for? To look deep inside and figure out what she wanted? She didn't think she needed or craved self-approval like some others might; she'd always generally had a high opinion of herself. Sometimes, it bothered her when others judged her and her lifestyle, but the more she'd matured, the more she realized that people judged what they didn't truly understand. She could spend her life trying to make people understand who she was and what she wanted, or she could just live.

Lola chose to just live.

But... still. There had to be some sort of message here for her. There were just too many incidents – too many mermaids popping up on her horizon – to call it coincidence. Automatically, Lola took a picture of the mirror and then moved on to the next display, her mind whirling.

Mermaid tarot cards.

Siren Island.

Prince's mermaid comb.

Mermaid mirror.

She needed to know more. Lola decided then and there she'd have a new project while on the island. Quite simply, she had to find a mermaid.

And hopefully, in the process, she'd find the answers to what she'd come here for.

CHAPTER 10

*L*ola spent the next hour devouring all the information she could find in the museum, but aside from a few of the mermaid myths and the artifacts, the rest of the information focused largely on the colonization of the island and its history of trade and produce. Luckily, the woman behind the desk had been able to point her toward a small gift shop and book store on-island, indicating they might have more information. Lola left, a thrum of excitement racing through her as she considered all the angles to her new project.

First, prove mermaids are real.

Second, find mermaids.

"No," Lola said out loud, half-laughing to herself as she stopped to examine some earrings in a window. She couldn't prove mermaids were real. It was more likely she just had to believe in them, and then they would show up. They had evaded any sort of true documentation for centuries, so it wasn't as though Lola was going to be the one to prove their existence to the world. Plus, did she really want that? She knew what it was like to have all eyes on her, judging her for being outside the norm, and could only imagine what the world would do to mermaids.

Scratch that, then.

First, believe in mermaids.

Second, find mermaids and what they mean to you.

There, Lola, thought, that's a little more focused. Plus, even if she never found a mermaid, god, they were gorgeous! To think of the art alone, the things she could create around a mermaid-themed show! Lola stopped in her tracks.

Could I curate that? Would it be worthwhile? What if I created art based solely on the lessons that mermaids are meant to teach us?

There was so much she wanted to do, Lola realized as she strolled the little cobblestone street with its brightly colored buildings lining both sides, people rolling by on bicycles and scooters. It was something she'd always struggled with, she supposed, focusing on just doing one thing when there were so many things a person could do. She never worried about money, because her needs were simple, and she was confident in her own ability to make money when she needed it, but she had never landed on one particular career path that could fully keep her invested.

Maybe it *was* time to bring all her interests under

one roof, Lola mused, as she found the small bookstore, tucked inside a brilliant turquoise building with a mural of an underwater scene painted on the side. Lola smiled as she studied it, and it wasn't until she took a step back that she saw that all the fish, reef, and coral pieces actually formed the face of a smiling woman, her hair twisting wildly behind her.

"Clever," Lola said, and automatically took a photo of it. Then she crossed the street to get out of the relentless sun, and ducked inside the cool bookstore. Taking a moment for her eyes to adjust, she smiled at a woman who greeted her from a chair in the corner, where she was adding beads to a colorful crochet project.

"Good day, may I help you?"

"I was pointed in your direction from the museum. She mentioned you might have books on mermaid mythology here?"

"That I do. An entire shelf full of them. You like mermaids?"

"It's hard not to, right? So beautiful and confident in their own right – masters of their domain."

"You'll find stories from all over the world, but if you're seeking out *our* mermaids, I suggest you read a few of the local books and some of the Caribbean-themed stories." The woman fluffed out her project in front of her, and despite herself, Lola walked closer to see.

"What are you working on?"

"It's a bikini top. I crochet them, just for fun, and

then add a few beads." She held it up, a brilliant red
bikini top with turquoise beads sewn in a floral pattern.
Lola was immediately smitten.

"I'LL BUY it from you, if it's for sale."

"Child, it's not finished yet."

"When will it be?"

"Mmm, not long now. You go look for your books
and I'll see what I can do. You just passing through or
will you be here a while?"

"I'm not sure," Lola said with a shrug as she crossed
to a small bookshelf painted the same turquoise color as
the outside of the building. "But then I never really am.
I like to take my time in places – if I need to stay longer,
I do, or I leave when I need to go. It all depends."

"A wanderer." The woman hummed.

"More or less. I like to think I'm more like a
connoisseur of the world. It's all so interesting to me
that I'm constantly fascinated by learning about new
places and cultures, the art, their stories… all of it."

"You're a photographer then?"

"I am, at times. I'm also a curator of art, I create
jewelry when the mood strikes, and I'm an interior
designer – depending on a client's needs."

"That's an interesting job. I bet you've had fun traveling the world."

"I have, though I've grown restless of late." Lola
shook her head and darted a glance at the woman over

her shoulder. "Sorry, I have no idea why I'm telling you that."

"People talk to me. It's what we do – sharing stories. I wouldn't run a bookstore if I didn't like to hear people's stories. But you take your time, look at a few of those books. I need to focus on finishing this up for you."

Dismissed, Lola realized, and smiled to herself as she scanned the shelf. The woman hadn't lied; there were numerous books from all over the world about mermaids, but she decided to take the woman's advice and focus on the local and regional books. Slim little volumes in ring binders, more likely made at home than from an actual printing press. Tugging a few out, she was happy to see they carried different sightings, as well as a variety of historical myths and interpretations of mermaid meanings.

"There now, I was closer than I thought. Try it on, just to be safe." The woman held the bikini up and gestured to a curtained corner of the room.

"I'm sure it's fine. It's adjustable, isn't it?"

"Try it on anyway. It's my work being advertised, and I like to make sure all my girls look good when they wear it."

It wasn't really an option, Lola realized. She placed her book selections on the counter by the register and took the swimming suit to the tiny dressing room in the corner. Hanging her camera on a hook in the wall, she closed the curtain around her and quickly undressed. She pulled the simple crocheted bottom on, thankful for its turquoise blue lining, and then tied the top around her breasts. Hoping everything was tucked in, as there were no mirrors in the fitting room, Lola stepped out into the bookstore.

"Well? What do you think?" Lola asked just as the door opened. Sunlight spilled into the bookstore from outside, casting the man who stepped inside as a shadow for a moment.

"I'll take it," Gage said, grinning at Lola from across the room, his eyes still hidden behind the mirrored glasses. Despite herself, Lola realized she really wanted to know what color his eyes were.

"It's not for sale to you," Lola said, allowing the double meaning to come through before shooting him a cheeky grin. "But I'm sure she can make you a male version."

Both women turned and eyed Gage appreciatively. Lola was delighted to see him actually squirm under their gazes.

"Mmmhmm. There's a few things I wouldn't mind seeing this boy in, but I don't think a crochet Speedo is one of them, and that's the honest truth of it." The woman chuckled and kissed Gage on both cheeks.

"I'm going to be shuddering over the imagery of a crochet Speedo the rest of the day," Gage promised, laughing with the woman. "Miss Maureen, you get lovelier every day."

"Of course I do." Miss Maureen chuckled at him

and Lola would've rolled her eyes if Miss Maureen didn't easily have twenty years on Gage.

"That's a real lovely swimming suit you've made this time," Gage said, turning back to scan Lola, and she could swear she felt heat rush through her under his appraisal. "I particularly like the peek-a-boo bits of turquoise you've worked in with the red. You'd be a fool not to buy it, Lola."

"Oh, I certainly plan to. It's surprisingly comfortable," Lola said, and beamed at Miss Maureen before tucking herself back behind the curtain and fanning her face for a moment. So much for playing it cool around Gage, she thought; the man had just seen her in about the skimpiest bikini she'd ever worn. Not much left to the imagination on that one, Lola mused. She quickly dressed again, unwinding her hair from its braid as it had all but come undone anyway. Shaking her waves out, she tucked the camera over her neck and stepped back out.

Gage glanced at her once more and paused, seeming as if he were about to speak. Then he shook his head and turned back to kiss Miss Maureen goodbye, his arms loaded with sodas and pamphlets.

"I'd say I hope the next time I see you is even more pleasant, but I'm not sure anything can top the joy of seeing you in one of Miss Maureen's creations."

"Go on with you now, Gage," Miss Maureen said before Lola could respond. "If you're going to flirt with the girl, you'd better do it properly and ask her on a real date."

"I tried, but she turned me down." Gage smiled.

Lola rolled her eyes. "It must be tough for your ego, I know."

"Try harder then." Miss Maureen shook her head sadly at the state of all men and moved behind the counter. "In the meantime, those sodas are getting warm and I need to make my sale."

"I'm gone," Gage said, shooting Lola one more smile before leaving the room.

"You sure about turning that fine man down?" Miss Maureen eyed Lola over the counter.

"I think so." Lola shrugged.

"Make him work for it, if you want it. Women come easily to him. Don't be one of those."

"Trust me, I read that loud and clear from the moment I got off the airplane and saw him surrounded by a gaggle of women."

"Mmm. I think you wear that bikini out, you'll find yourself a gaggle of men. I did a great job with that one, if I do say so myself." Miss Maureen chuckled and rang up Lola's purchases, tucking them into a reusable canvas bag.

"Saves the reefs, you know. Plastic bags are bad for our turtles. They think they're jellyfish and eat them." Miss Maureen made a sad noise as she pursed her lips.

"You're smart to offer the reusable ones, then," Lola

said, hoisting her bag in thanks. "I'll be back after I get through these books."

"Wonderful. I'll make you something else. Now that I've seen how my work looks on you, I've a mind for another project."

"The mind of an artist..." Lola smiled from the doorway. "It's always busy."

"That it is, my dear, that it is." Lola could tell that Miss Maureen was pleased at being called an artist, and she made a note to stop back in at the end of the week.

CHAPTER 11

*A*rmed with her books, her new bikini, and a large Tervis tumbler filled with the makings for a Dark & Stormy, Lola headed toward the beach at the Laughing Mermaid. She'd found a small place to rent a scooter and had made a few rounds of the little downtown before the thought of her lovely B&B called to her, making her itch to get in the water.

The beach at the Laughing Mermaid was quiet, though she'd heard the voices of other guests earlier that day. They must all be out on excursions, Lola thought, before taking a quick sip of her drink and eyeing the ocean. Yup, she definitely needed to take a dip before she settled in to read.

Leaving her stuff on a lounge chair, Lola sauntered down to the ocean, enjoying the feel of the sand under her feet. It was almost too hot to walk on, seeming to push her to get to the water faster. Once at the waves,

Lola looked around, admiring the crystal-clear water, and how the blue seemed to change from turquoise to cobalt and back again. The ocean was a moody one, as Lola well knew – it was one of the reasons she was always drawn to water wherever she went.

Sighing in pure joy, Lola slipped beneath the surface, closing her eyes as the water enveloped her, seeming to welcome her home. It was one of the reasons she'd gotten her scuba certification years before. There was something about floating in the ocean, where no one could talk to her, that heightened her senses and made her feel at peace with the world. Being in the ocean was like meditation for Lola, and she always craved it when she was away from water for too long. She'd have to stop by a dive shop while she was here, Lola thought as she surfaced, pushing her hair from her face and floating lightly in the buoyant water.

What would it be like to call the sea your home? Lola wondered as she paddled about. The water was the perfect temperature – just refreshing enough, not so cold as to send her scurrying out. She wondered how weird it would be to look out onto land but not be able to join in that world. Indulging herself in the fantasy of being a mermaid, Lola floated for a while before she turned to see two women walk into the garden and stop under a palm tree, waving out at her in the water.

Lola waved back and floated for a few more moments before the sunshine and her cocktail beckoned. Getting out of the water, she shook her hair out and

strolled up the beach to where the two women –
gorgeous women at that – chattered to each other in the
garden. These must be the infamous Mirra and Jolie.
She'd heard about them from Sam, and Lola had to
conclude that Sam was right. These women were seriously stunning. Even as confident as she was in her
looks and her body, Lola found herself drawn to these
two. Something special seemed to shimmer around
them, an effervescent sparkle in the air, and Lola imagined that every eye in the room would be on these two
wherever they went.

"You must be Lola," the dark-haired one said,
standing up and holding out her hand.

"Of course it's Lola. Sam's told us enough about
her." The blonde woman rose and held out her arms.
"I'm a hugger, sorry."

"I don't mind," Lola laughed, and embraced both
women, making a mental note of the hum of energy she
felt from them, similar to the one she had noticed from
Irma. The blonde, Mirra, was wrapped in an airy white
sarong, and Jolie, the dark-haired one, was in a
screaming orange bikini. Both looked equally appealing,
and Lola wondered why there wasn't a line of men sali-
vating at the door.

"It's nice to finally meet you both," Lola said.
"Sam's spoken very highly of you both – well, and of
Irma too. I really appreciate how you've stepped in and
become like a family for her. She needs it."

Jolie eyed Lola as she wrapped a towel around her

body and settled into her chair, sliding her sunglasses on again against the brightness of the Caribbean sun.

"I'd say Lucas has provided that for her more than anyone has, but we love Sam and are happy to have her as a neighbor," Jolie said. "It sounds like you're really her main person in life. Are you coming down to make sure we're good enough?"

"Oh, stop it, Jolie, you can't just assume the worst of everyone. I'm sure Lola's protective of Sam, but also knows she's a grown woman." Mirra shot an apologetic look at Lola.

"Actually, I'm here because a tarot card reader in Italy handed me a pack of mermaid tarot cards and basically told me to travel here. But, yes, I've been meaning to come visit Sam and make sure she's doing okay down here. From the sounds of it, she's flourishing."

"She really is, isn't she?" Jolie beamed, attitude forgotten in their shared protectiveness over Sam.

"From what I can tell, she's over-the-moon happy. Which makes me happy. That's all I need to know." Lola shrugged and took a sip of her cocktail, enjoying the spiciness of the dark rum.

"See? That's a good friend," Mirra pointed out.

"I have to tell you both, I absolutely adore what you did for decorations in my room. It's truly delightful. I may have to get some ideas from you for clients of mine."

"Okay, I officially like you," Jolie decided and

settled back in her chair, causing Lola to laugh. "Tell me more about how much you like it."

"I really, truly do. I appreciate it when there's a touch of whimsy or emotion added to a room. It's nice when places take time to infuse some personality into their accommodations. Otherwise, you'd just be at any other chain hotel around the world."

"We do like to differentiate ourselves from some of the more basic hotels," Mirra agreed.

"You have a real gem here," Lola said.

"Sam tells us you're an artist of some sort? Is that correct? She made it sound like you're basically her complete opposite." Mirra laughed and twirled a lock of long blonde hair around her finger. "Sort of a Bohemian globetrotter who does a little bit of everything."

"That's a fairly accurate description, I suppose." Lola laughed and took another sip of her drink, stretching her legs out in front of her and moving her books to the table beside her. "My mother is an art curator as well, and she'd pick me up and haul me all over the world with her. For which I'm grateful. It's helped me in my career, and following my own interests, but I can't say I'm as focused as some would like me to be."

"Do you care about those who say such things?" Jolie inquired.

"Not particularly," Lola said, and they all laughed.

Jolie leaned over and picked up one of her books,

flipping through the pages. "Are you interested in mermaids?" She shot Mirra a look and held up the book.

"I mean, it's kind of hard not to be, right? They're so damn fascinating. I went to town today and stopped at the museum, took some time learning about the history here. The woman there sent me on to the bookstore."

"That's Miss Maureen's bikini!" Jolie exclaimed. "I was going to ask you where you got it; it looked familiar. She doesn't sell those to just anyone, you know. You should be happy she did. It looks fantastic on you."

"Thanks. I didn't go there for a bikini, but it's really an interesting piece," Lola admitted, looking down at the blue beads shimmering against the red threads. "She was really nice and had some good books on mermaids."

"We have some more, as well, once you're done with those," Mirra offered.

"Oh, great! I don't know why, but it seems to be a bit of a theme that keeps popping up for me. So now I'm just surrendering to the inevitable." Lola shrugged.

The sisters glanced at each other. "And what theme is that?"

"Oh, that I have to hunt them down."

"You're going to hunt mermaids?" Jolie's voice sharpened.

"No, no, no. Not like hunt them as in try to find and kill them." Lola chuckled. "But just... satisfy my curiosity. There's art to be found with the mermaids, and I'm not yet sure what form that will take for me.

Perhaps I'll get some creative inspiration from the symbology and lessons that we can learn from mermaids, or if by some amazing chance I ever see one in person, maybe I could photograph or paint her. But it's just kind of enthralled me since I arrived, and now I want to know more."

"Mermaid art is exceptionally popular," Mirra said, and shot a warning glance at Jolie, who had started to open her mouth. "People have been deriving inspiration from their mythologies for centuries."

"I know. Maybe it's just a strong draw because we're in a time where women need to feel more empowered, but the idea of mermaids and their confidence is really appealing to me. I'd like to explore it more."

"Well, this is certainly the place to do so," Jolie said, tossing her dark hair over her shoulder and moving her chair a bit to angle in the sun better.

"Do you have any suggestions on where to start? Aside from my books, that is?"

"There's a mermaid statue out by the cliffs on the west end of the island. They say that's where Nalachi lost his life, and now you'll hear a mermaid sing during the storms there. There's also some caves in the cliffs where you could look for some of the old rock drawings. You have to go by boat, though," Mirra said.

"And for a longer trip, there's a small uninhabited island not far off the coast here. Your only access is at low tide, and you have to hire the right kind of boat to get close to shore. The rumor is that's where the most mermaid artifacts have been found," Jolie added.

"Really? That's perfect. Do you recommend I start with one over the other?"

"Maybe just the easier excursion to the caves to start. You can do that in a few hours. I feel like the island is more of a day trip, where you want to pack a picnic and such."

"Great! Now all I have do is rent a boat. Is there anyone you recommend, where I can rent something like a Zodiac?"

"Oh – we absolutely do not recommend that you go out on your own," Jolie said. "In fact, we insist on it. However, we can arrange a private charter boat for you. I'll go in and make the call."

"Is it really expensive?" Lola asked.

"No, I think for the small boat it's not too bad. I'll get a final price for you," Jolie said and strolled away.

"What should I expect from the caves? Or look for? How did a mermaid statue get out there?" Lola asked Mirra.

"In the caves, you'll want to bring a light. Do you have a dive light or something like that? If not, we have some you can use. You'll want to head fairly far into the cave – wear water shoes – and you'll find all sorts of old drawings etched on the walls. It's quite cool, actually. And I'm not really certain on the statue. I feel like you'll find history on that in one of the books."

"Is a seven thirty start time okay for you?" Jolie called down from the house.

"Perfect."

"A hundred dollars for the whole day?"

"Even better."

"They'll be here to pick you up in the morning."

CHAPTER 12

*L*ola rose early enough to see the sun rise, wandering out to the ocean while the B&B was still quiet to do some yoga on the beach and to start the day with a clear head. She'd spent another lovely night in the swing chair on her balcony, sipping her Dark & Stormy, a delicious concoction of dark rum and ginger beer, and devouring her newly acquired mermaid books. By the time she went to bed, her mind was swimming with possibilities as to what direction she should focus on for her art project.

Mainly, though? It seemed like mermaids carried different messages for different people. She'd mused over that thought during her yoga, wondering how mermaids chose whom to reveal themselves to. Or maybe those who felt drawn to mermaid lore needed to hear certain messages from them. Of everything she had learned about the mermaids the night before, the theme that resonated the most strongly was that of the divine feminine power. Which was something that Lola absolutely could get behind. It would be interesting to explore what the divine feminine power meant for each person, as it was a broad area. Certainly there were the more traditional forms of beauty, but what about physical strength? Or vulnerability?

Looking forward to her boat trip, Lola packed a waterproof knapsack the girls had given her, along with a dive light, and made sure she had reef-safe sunscreen, sturdy water shoes, her waterproof camera – no trusty Leica today – and an apple and a few granola bars. Lola filled her reusable water bottle, her favorite purchase from Costa Rica years ago, now covered with stickers from around the world. Then she slipped into her bikini, pulled a tank and sarong over it, and braided her hair into loose pigtails before donning a simple straw hat. Happy to have a plan for the day, she texted Sam what she was doing and went downstairs to wait for the charter company.

It shouldn't have surprised her when Gage's truck turned in front of the house, but somehow it still did. A flush crept through Lola, and she realized that she'd thought more about him at odd moments during the day yesterday than she would have liked. She'd done her best to push him from her mind, reminding herself that this trip was about her and ignoring the naughty voice in her head that insisted Gage could also be about her needs. He was not the distraction she wanted right now.

He can just be a friend, Lola thought, and reminded herself that men weren't just good for sex. Some had other useful attributes, like friendship or building things.

"So you did decide to take me up on my offer of showing you around the island," Gage said, getting out of the truck and rounding the front. Today he wore loose swim trunks, a fitted dark tank that showcased his very well-defined abs, a Red Sox baseball cap, and – once again – his mirrored aviators. Lola did her best not to drool, and ignored the voice that insisted she get in line to ride this ride.

"Actually you can blame Jolie for that one. I just told her I needed a boat chartered. Which is what you do, then, I assume?" Lola asked, handing him her bag and climbing into the front seat.

"Among other things," Gage said as he shifted the truck into gear.

"I suppose that explains the large groups of women thronging around you all the time," Lola said, tapping her finger on her lips as she studied him.

"Nope, that's just the norm," Gage said, straight-faced.

Lola couldn't help but chuckle. "Naturally," she said. "So, you're a boat guy? Do you run daily charters or snorkel tours?"

"A little bit of this and that. I don't like to overbook myself, so I'll pick and choose tour times. About twice a week I'll take a large group out on my bigger boat, and there we offer everything from snorkeling and a catered lunch to music and a sunset cocktail tour. It just depends on what the clients are looking for. For smaller charters, like today's, I have some small boats to suit those needs."

"Have you been captaining all your life?"

"Not even close." Gage laughed, reaching up to tug at the leather cord tying his hair back, and Lola wondered at the sheepishness he showed there. "In another life I was an attorney."

"Is that so? A shark, huh? You don't practice anymore at all?"

Another tug on the hair.

"Here and there. When the locals need some help, I offer it for free. Their laws are a bit different than ours, so I just do my best to guide where I can."

"What kind of law?"

"In-house counsel for a production company. Mainly movies and made-for-TV movies."

"Shut up – like the Hallmark Channel and stuff?" Lola asked, delighted.

"What is it with you women and the Hallmark Channel?"

"I think we just like the consistency of knowing we can watch a movie where the local baker in his Christmas sweater wins the girl. It's sweet to see a nice guy win for once, I guess." Lola shrugged.

"Hey, I'm all for it. There's nothing wrong with watching something that has a happy ending or makes you feel good inside. Entertainment is so subjective."

"Have you met a lot of famous people?"

"Not as many as you'd think. They kept us grunts up in the offices and away from the beautiful people. Probably scared their agents would try to renegotiate contracts once they set eyes on the attorneys."

"It sounds quite interesting. Why'd you stop?"

Another tug on the hair, Lola noted. Interesting. He wasn't as comfortable talking about himself as she'd thought a guy like him would be. She'd met men before who exuded the same level of machismo as Gage did, and they seemed to never shut up about themselves and their accomplishments.

"Ah, I'm not entirely sure, to be honest. I didn't hate the work. Admittedly, we were an incredibly busy company so there were a lot of demands on my time. But I was in Ft. Lauderdale for a meeting one day and was walking the streets, as I often did when I had a case issue on my mind, and I saw a boatyard. Walked over, and met a man named Mack who refused to sell me a boat until I took some classes. Once I did, I was hooked. It wasn't much longer after that I left the company and off I went, with no particular destination in mind."

"That's amazing. Not many people have the guts to do that. It's a huge change to leave a stable income and travel with no set destination. I'm liking you more and more, Gage," Lola said with a laugh as they pulled to a stop in the parking lot of a boatyard. "I like when people take the time to shake their lives up and change the status quo. It makes for a far less boring life."

"I can't deny that. It's been quite the ride," Gage admitted, rounding the car and hefting a cooler over his shoulder, as well as a large waterproof bag.

"How'd you pick Siren Island?" Lola asked, falling in step next to him. The floating dock swayed gently beneath their feet as they walked to a small boat with a shaded top.

"I think it picked me, to be honest," Gage said. He tossed the bag into the back of the boat, along with the cooler, before hopping in and reaching a hand out for her bag.

"I can see that. It would fit with her legend. She calls to people as sirens do." Lola laughed as Gage held out a hand to help her step into the boat. Just as her foot touched down, the boat swayed, causing her to bump against Gage's decidedly hard chest. Lola sighed, tamping down the immediate desire that rose in her, and reminded herself – again – that he was to be just a friend.

"You okay there?" Gage asked, steadying her and looking down at her. Lola hadn't realized how tall he was until he stood over her and she had to tilt her head back to look at him.

"All good. Sorry about that. Where do you want me?" Lola asked, looking around at the boat.

"Since it's just us, you can take the seat beside the captain's chair," Gage said, pointing to her seat. Lola perched in the seat while she watched Gage work, storing the bag away, strapping the cooler down, and checking all the safety equipment and fuel on the boat. Once he'd gone through his checklist, he looked over at her.

"Ready to head out?"

"Aye, Captain."

CHAPTER 13

*I*t was one of those rare perfect mornings, where the water was almost like glass, and the wind was next to nonexistent. The sun peeked out behind a swath of fuzzy clouds on the horizon, blanketing the sea in a warm honey hue as they motored quietly from the marina and out to sea. Lola let the silence hang between them, content with looking out at the water and back to where the island was beginning to shake itself awake.

They rode companionably for a while, neither feeling the need to break the beauty of the morning with chatter, and Lola found herself liking Gage even more. There was a time for making conversation and a time for appreciating the beauty of the world around them.

"Look," Gage whispered, seeming to understand Lola's need for calm this morning, and pointed to the port side of the boat. Lola squinted and then gasped when a dolphin broke the surface, blowing a small puff of air from its blowhole before diving once more under the smooth surface of the sea.

"Dolphins!" Lola exclaimed. "Can we go closer?"

"Sure. They love to interact with the waves from the boat," Gage said. He increased their speed until they were close to the pod, but maintained a respectful distance, allowing the dolphins to approach by their own choice. When several surfaced close to the boat, leaping in the waves, Lola cheered.

"Oh my gosh! They have a baby with them!" Lola exclaimed. She rushed to the front of the boat to lean over the bow, camera in hand, to capture the way the small dolphin raced alongside its mother, jumping from the water in joy. Lola's heart danced in her chest as she watched them play in the waves, dipping and diving at their own whims. In moments, they dove deep and swam on, heading in a different direction than where Gage turned the boat. Despite herself, Lola waved goodbye to the pod.

"I'm not sure they saw that," Gage chuckled.

"Oh, what a beautiful experience," Lola breathed, happy to have grabbed a few shots on her camera. "The baby was absolutely darling. Do you ever stop and get in the water with them?"

"Sometimes, but not if there is a baby, no. I think they're more protective of the baby, and by the time you get in the water, they'll just swim right off. They are loads of fun to be in the sea with, though, if they do decide to stick around and play."

"What a gift," Lola said, leaning back in the chair and kicking her legs up on the dash. She saw Gage give them a glance but ignored the thrum of energy that pulsed between them. "I'll take that as a positive sign on my quest."

"And just what quest is that?"

"To find a mermaid, naturally." Lola boomed out a laugh when she saw Gage's skeptical look.

"If you find me a mermaid today, I'll kiss you," Gage finally said, and Lola shook her head at him.

"If I find a mermaid today, I'll likely kiss you as well. Could you imagine? I know it sounds silly, and I doubt I'll actually find one – because you know, they probably aren't real – but at the very least, I'd like to do some more research on the historical references to them around the island."

"Ah, so that's why you want to go to the Wishing Caves," Gage said, standing comfortably at the wheel, his eyes on the horizon.

"Is that their name? I wonder why…" Lola turned her eyes to the horizon, where jagged cliffs jutted into the sky at the end of the island.

"It was said, back in the day, that if you were able to get into the caves on a low tide, present an offering, and make your wish or prayer, it would indeed come true. But you see, without a boat or strong navigational skills, it's incredibly tricky to get into the caves."

"And you can't access them from the surface?"

"Not unless you rappel down and rock-climb your way back up. Some do, but it's not a common point of entry."

"So they're relatively untouched? Jolie and Mirra mentioned some cave drawings."

"They're pretty much as pristine as could be. Locals don't go there; too superstitious. And few boat operators will risk their boats among the rocks."

"But you don't worry?"

"No, I have a good eye. Plus, I've got you as a lookout."

"Oh really? Who said I was going to work on this charter?" Lola shot him a saucy look.

"I do. If you want to see your caves, that is."

"Fair enough," Lola laughed. "I've never minded getting my hands dirty. What do you need from me?"

"Go up front and lay on the boat, so your head is just in front and you can see the rocks. I'll need you to give me warning of any rock that's too close. As we get closer I'll just pull the motor up and row us the rest of the way."

"A true adventure," Lola said, moving to the front of the boat as they neared the cliffs. They were much larger than she had anticipated from afar, and as they drew close she realized why so few people came here. First, there was no discernable cave entrance that she could see from the water. Secondly, there was a large circle of jagged rocks that poked from the water, and even from her vantage point, Lola couldn't see where they would enter. It was only when Gage slowed the boat and steered it past a particularly large boulder that she saw the slim passage in the rocks that would allow access to shore.

"I'm going to go as slow as I can until I have to row," Gage said. "Keep alert."

"Aye, Captain," Lola called cheerfully. She kept her eyes trained on the brilliant blue water below her, calling out any dangers in their path until they rounded the precipice. Then Gage cut the engine and pulled it up from the water.

"I'll row from here."

"Gage… wow. This is seriously beautiful," Lola breathed. Tucked back behind the circle of rocks was a stunning private beach, protected on both sides by cliff walls, with brilliant white sand and not a soul to be seen.

"I know. It's like this secret wonder that nobody knows about. I love that there's all this beauty hidden back here. I feel like the best spots are often the toughest to find," Gage said, paddling them lightly toward shore until the hull of the boat bumped lightly against the sand. He hopped easily from the boat, walking around to the front where Lola still lay, and gently tugged the boat further up on the sand to secure it.

"All good?" Lola asked, rolling to put her feet on the floor.

"Yes, ma'am, all good. You may disembark," Gage

said, rounding the boat and grabbing the cooler from the back, as well as Lola's bag. Taking them higher up on the sand, he came to the back and held his hands up for her. When Lola went to give him hers, he just put his hands on her waist and lifted her easily out. Did she notice his hard body as she slid lightly down it before her toes touched the sand? Damn straight she did. Did she notice the palpable hum of chemistry that sizzled between their bodies like a live wire? Absolutely. She wondered if Gage felt it, or if he was so used to women fawning all over him that he no longer paid attention.

"Thanks for the lift, cutie," Lola said, and bent to swing her knapsack onto her shoulder. She began heading up toward the beach, where she could just now make out the entrance to the cave. "Honestly, how did anyone ever find this? It's barely visible from the sea."

"Pirates did at one point, which doesn't surprise me. They're notorious for finding hidey holes along the coast."

"Oh – maybe we'll find treasure," Lola laughed as she dug in her bag for her dive light and her water shoes. "Okay, fearless captain, shall I lead the way, or do you know the route?"

"Let me go in first. That way I'll sweep any creepy crawlies out of the way for you," Gage said, sliding a camping light onto his baseball cap and strapping a dive knife to his ankle.

"What do you think you'll need a knife for?" Lola asked, eyes round.

"It's more for if we get entangled than needing to kill anything. I suspect the only thing we'll find in here are bats. Which we like, I must tell you as an islander, because they eat the mosquitos."

"Ah, yes. Then I too am a fan of bats," Lola said, following him as he scrambled up some loose rocks until he stood at the mouth of the cave.

"You're not one of those girls who screams at bats and worries about her hair?"

Lola pointed to the massive braids on her head and laughed. "I have plenty of hair; if I lose some to a bat, so be it. I'd be more worried about terrifying the poor things."

Gage nodded his approval before sliding his glasses off and tucking them in a pouch. Instantly intrigued, Lola went closer and peered up at his face until he tilted his head at her in question.

"What? Do I have something on my face?"

"I've just never seen you with your sunglasses off. I wondered what color eyes you have," Lola said – and then mentally kicked herself. Could she be more transparent in letting Gage know she'd been thinking about him?

"Green – like money, my co-workers used to say, but now I prefer to say like the palm trees."

They were a brilliant green, and Lola let herself indulge in a small sigh. It was just so unfair; didn't this man have any faults? A gorgeous face, entrancing emerald eyes, and a body cut from rock. No wonder every woman for miles was swooning over him.

"Yes, I'd say more like palm trees. Do they change color? When you're angry? Mine do that sometimes, depending on my mood."

"I don't know. I'm not usually looking in the mirror when I'm angry." Gage laughed and turned, clicking his light on and ducking his head into the entrance of the cave. Lola followed him in silence, decidedly ignoring the way his swim trunks bunched around his delightfully strong bum, and instead shone her light against the walls looking for drawings.

"It's cool in here. But there's still a breeze," Lola said.

"That means there's an outlet somewhere else in the cave. Which would make sense for the bats to come in and out. I don't suggest you shine your light on the ceiling, as you'll startle them. Let's leave them to their rest."

That was when she heard it.

The rustling of thousands of bats, busy even at rest, and a few flitting by her head.

"Oh man, you didn't say how many there'd be," Lola breathed, coming close to Gage and peering up where the light from the front of the cave shone on the bats. "That's so beautiful. Just look at them all!"

"I know. Usually people hate bats, but I'm so fascinated by them. They're like little flying monkeys or something."

"Like the monkeys in *The Wizard of Oz*?"

"Mmm, I like to think friendlier."

"Let's hope so, or we're screwed."

"I doubt that we'll be taken down by a bat apocalypse, but if so? Yes, we're screwed."

"Let's not talk about getting screwed in this cave. I mean… do you even have cell reception out here? What happens if there's an emergency?" Lola wondered aloud as they picked their way through the tunnel. It continued to narrow before banking sharply to the left. Now they were relying solely upon their lights. Lola's heart began to pick up with excitement – or nerves, she couldn't tell which.

"I'll be your hero, little one, don't you worry," Gage said easily, his focus on the path ahead of him. "Plus, it's not too much longer now… ah! Here we are."

Gage stopped so quickly that Lola bumped into his back before she could stop herself. Reaching behind himself with one arm, Gage pulled her around so that she stood in front of him, his hands on her shoulders.

"Look."

CHAPTER 14

"Oh... oh my," Lola said, stepping forward involuntarily, her light shining on the wall in front of them. "I had no idea there'd be so many."

"I'm certain there's more hidden deeper in the caves, but I've never had time to explore further. Usually, I stop at this room because the people I'm with aren't comfortable going deeper."

"I mean... I'm happy to go deeper, but you need to give me a minute here first. These are seriously amazing," Lola said, already enchanted as she stepped in front of a large wall covered in various drawings in a chalky red paint and some sort of black tar substance.

"Is that tar?"

"It looks like it. Or a substance similar to it. It's stood the test of time in here," Gage said, coming to stand beside her.

"It's like they're telling a story," Lola mused,

shining her light up the damp wall to where two rudi-
mentary figures danced around what looked like a fire.
The next scene showed a passionate embrace. From
there, the scenes flowed into the sea, where a mermaid
was finally introduced. Lola hovered in front of the first
mermaid drawing and held her hand out.

Gage grabbed it. "Don't touch."

"I'm not, I promise. I just wanted to…" Lola trailed
off, distracted by the pulse of energy between their
hands. How could she explain to him that she'd only
wanted to feel the energy of the drawing without
sounding like a whackadoodle?

"See if you could feel anything?" Gage guessed,
accurately, and dropped her hand.

"Yes, I know it sounds silly." Lola laughed and held
her hand in front of the mermaid etching. There was
nothing at first, but when she closed her eyes… there it
was. A small punch of energy, so pure in its joy that
Lola couldn't help but beam.

"I'm guessing that's a yes?" Gage asked, watching
her.

"It's beautiful," Lola murmured, and moved on,
following the story she'd learned about in the museum.

"Do you think he drew this? Nalachi?"

"He died, remember?" Gage pointed to one of the
last scenes, where it looked like a mermaid and two
mermaid babies carried a body beneath the waves.

"The mermaids came. In here? And drew this? Of
course they did," Lola said, holding her hand over the

scene with the body. This one pulsed with such an intense sadness that Lola closed her eyes for a moment, willing the tears back.

"It seems to end on a happy note, however," Gage said, pointing to the last scene, where the mermaid and her babies danced in the water, warning a boat away from the rocks. When Lola held up her hand to that one, she did feel happiness, but laced with sorrow. She could understand that. She wondered if anyone ever felt deeply happy again after a great loss, or if it was always tinged with a hint of sorrow. Or perhaps that was simply the human condition – happiness and sorrow hand in hand, not a soul exempt from feeling either.

"It's happy, but a different type of happiness," Lola said, turning to look at Gage. "Maybe even... more happy for knowing the pain of loss?"

"Perhaps. A 'savor the best of life's moments' feeling?" Gage asked, his eyes holding hers. The moment drew out – a beat, then two – before Lola broke the gaze and turned back to the paintings.

"Thank you for bringing me here. I'd like to take a few photos. Would you mind helping me by holding the light near them? I don't want to set off a flash in here and scare the bats."

"Your wish is my command," Gage said, and Lola laughed, shaking her head at him over her shoulder.

"If that was a wish, I'd be upset with myself. If I'm in a wishing cave, I need a much better wish."

"I'll say, *At your service, ma'am,* instead then. Do

you want to go further into the cave? You can make your wish anywhere you want."

"I'd like that," Lola said, concentrating on taking as many photos as she could in the light of Gage's lamp. She didn't mind if they weren't perfectly focused; the pictures were only for her – well, and maybe Sam. This felt too private to share to the world. Which reminded her...

"I haven't seen any photos of these drawings at the museum or in any of the books. Is there a reason for that?"

"I don't really know. Maybe nobody's taken the time to record them? You could be the first."

"Mmmm, I don't think I'm comfortable with that. This feels private to me." Lola gestured to the wall of drawings. "As though a woman poured out her love story in art form. I don't know how I'd feel sharing that with the world."

"What will you do with the photos then?"

"They're for me. For inspiration down the road, I suppose. I'll show Sam, my best friend who lives here, but otherwise, I've no need to profit from this. Some things are best left just as they are. Plus, I like that this is secretive and hard to get to. As soon as hordes of tourists find a spot, someone inevitably does something stupid. We'd lose this beautiful treasure."

"I can appreciate your sensibilities," Gage said, leading her down another small tunnel. "Not everyone carries the same view. I like that about you, Lola. I also like that you're not afraid of bats, that you can feel energy from rocks, and that you haven't complained once about getting dirty."

A dangerous hum filled Lola's blood, and she tried to ignore the low pull of lust that made her want to tell this man all the things she liked about him, as well as what she'd like to do with him. *Just because a man compliments you doesn't mean he wants to sleep with you*, Lola gently chided herself.

"Well, thank you, Gage," she said, keeping her tone light. "I wouldn't have asked to go caving if I was afraid of getting dirty."

"You'd be surprised," Gage bit out.

Lola laughed again and then came to a stop when they rounded a corner into a large cavern. Across the room was a pillar of rocks, built upon one another, with light from a small hole in the ceiling filtering down so that rays illuminated it.

"An altar," Lola declared and scampered past Gage to stand before it, looking down at the top stone. Cylindrical, almost like a small bowl, the rock had a deep well in it where items could be placed. At the center was a single mermaid etching. It would be impossible to ignore the energy that pulsed from this altar.

"Do you feel it?" Gage asked at her ear.

"Of course; do you?"

"Yes, just a bit. I didn't in front of the paintings, but here… yes, I can tell there's something in the air." Gage held up his hand and passed it over the top of the altar. "Almost like dipping my hand into water."

"It's a good energy," Lola said. "Much like how the ocean calls you home."

"Is that where you belong?" Gage teased.

"Isn't that where you belong? You're the one who up and bought a boat and moved here."

"True, I've always felt at peace around water. I suppose it does feel like home to me now," Gage agreed.

"I'm the same. Everywhere I travel, I instinctively find myself seeking out the sea as soon as I can. It's good for me."

"Maybe you're a mermaid."

"Wouldn't that be something?" It was the second time in as many days that someone had suggested it. Though Lola dismissed it as ridiculous, a part of her wanted to dance around in joy at the thought.

"It looks like a few people who did venture here left gifts along the way." Gage had crossed behind the altar to a wall, where Lola could now see a few small bundles of items.

"What's there?"

"Combs, some wooden beads, tools... a little bit of everything. Honestly, some of this stuff should be in museums," Gage said. Lola appreciated that he kept his hands to himself and didn't touch the items, seeming to understand that would be wrong.

"Better they stay here. We don't want to ruin somebody's wishes," Lola said. A wish was someone's hopes and dreams, and to take that away – well, it just didn't sit right with her either.

"Will you make a wish?"

"I'd like to, yes, if you don't mind giving me a little space."

"No problem," Gage said, nodding his head toward the other side of the large cavern. "I'll just go take a look at the walls over here and see if I can find any other drawings."

Lola stood before the altar and closed her eyes, sliding a simple twisted gold band from her finger. She'd had it for ages – picked up on a jaunt through Egypt, and she'd worn it more or less ever since. While she'd miss its weight on her finger, she didn't think it would be appropriate to make a wish in a mermaid wishing cave with something that held little value for her.

There were always sacrifices on the path to dreams.

Taking a deep breath, Lola closed her eyes and placed the ring in the dish on the altar. She spent some time calming her mind, letting the energy of the cave, the ocean, and all time flow through her until she could get clear on what she would wish for. As a relatively content woman, her needs were few.

I wish to find what it is that I'm searching for.

There, Lola thought, that was an appropriate wish. For she'd always been confident in herself and her choices in life, but there was still... something. A restlessness that she had yet to come to terms with. Perhaps that was just who she was, but her gut told her that she'd been seeking something her whole life.

Or someone.

The words were like a whisper floating through the cave. Lola whirled around, but Gage was busy studying a wall, politely giving her space, and nobody else was there. Shaking her head, Lola looked back at where her ring glinted in the light from the ceiling. Running her finger over it, she said goodbye.

"I'm finished, thank you," Lola called.

Gage turned to walk toward her, but stopped so suddenly, his mouth going slack-jawed, that Lola had to turn to see if something was behind her.

"What's wrong?"

"Ahh, it's nothing. Really. I think just an illusion from the light. Are you set? Happy with your wish?"

"I am. Will you make one?" Lola asked.

"Um… you know what? Why not?" Gage shrugged, and stepped to the altar, his eyes drawn to the ring in the bowl. "You gave your pretty ring?"

"I guess I figured that something as important as a wish deserved a worthy offering."

Gage eyed her for a moment before nodding, then reached up to slip a chain from his neck and dropped it into the bowl. Lola was dying to ask him what he'd left, but decided to give him the same privacy he'd afforded her. She crossed the room to study a few smaller etchings on the wall.

She knew when he'd made his wish. It was like someone throwing a penny in the fountain, and the ripple of water rolling away from where the penny entered the water. But instead of water, it was energy that rolled over her, and Lola absorbed it, completely in love with the beauty of this cave and the mystical magick found here.

"All done."

"Thank you for bringing me here." Lola turned, looking up at him, emotion bringing a hitch to her voice. "It's truly one of the most powerful places I've ever visited."

"You're welcome. Thank you for coming with me. I've never had the opportunity to experience this space in this way, let alone to explore deeper. You're an excellent companion."

"And you're an excellent captain," Lola said, then gave him an embarrassed look when her stomach rumbled loudly.

"Time for lunch?"

"That it is," Lola chuckled and followed him to the tunnel leading from the cave. Turning back, she looked at the altar. It stood just as she'd seen it when she entered, the light filtering lazily down from the ceiling. And yet, it was different now in some way – as if a rosy hue glowed around the altar. Too enthralled to take a photo, Lola captured the image with her mind, determined to recreate it in her art later on.

"Coming along?"

"I'm coming! I hope you like granola bars, because that's about all I have."

"Silly woman, a gentleman never takes a lady on a date without planning for food."

A little thrill ran through her at the word 'date.' This certainly wasn't one, as she was paying him for his charter services, but she took his teasing in stride.

"A gentleman? Show me where he is!"

Gage's laugh echoed off the wall and despite herself, Lola smiled the whole way out.

CHAPTER 15

*G*age watched as Lola all but scampered out of the cave, delighted to be back on the beach, and whipped her clothes off. His mind drew a blank for a full fifteen seconds, then he gulped against his suddenly-dry throat.

She wore the same bikini from the other day, the one Miss Maureen – god bless her soul – had designed. It couldn't get much skimpier, and yet Lola strolled casually to the beach, the triangle of fabric barely covering her very generous bum, and Gage had to turn away for a moment and adjust his shorts before he found himself in a very awkward position. Bending to busy himself with the cooler, he only glanced over when she called to him.

"The water feels amazing. You should get in!"

And when a mermaid invites you to get in the water, you go, Gage thought. He pulled his shirt over his head, completely entranced by Lola – as he'd been since the day she'd glared at him across the airport. He'd noticed her immediately, the confident curvy woman striding through customs with only a leather pack and a tote bag on her shoulder. Tumbled reddish curls, eyes he'd later learned were hazel green, and more than enough curves to keep a man's hands busy for days – yeah, Gage had been lost. He'd had a few distressing nights since he'd met Lola, waking covered in sweat, her name on his lips.

She had glowed at the altar.

When he'd turned around to ask her if she was done with her wish, she'd been glowing. Perhaps it was a trick of the eyes, from looking with his headlamp to her standing in the ray of light shining from the hole above, but she'd been lit up in a rose-gold hue that had almost brought him to his knees. When a goddess shows herself, one should kneel. He wanted her more than anything he'd wanted in his life. Which made him want to tread carefully, for Lola struck him as someone who was… well, was like him. Comfortable in her own skin, used to moving on from lovers, and confident in being alone. As desperately as he wanted to taste every inch of her body, he worried that was all he'd get.

He'd given his necklace away, the one his mother had given him to protect him on his travels. Gage had worn it always, but now he wondered if he'd protected himself too much, keeping busy with work, never forming attachments too deeply. What he wanted now, he deeply feared had already slipped by.

Lola grinned at him from where she treaded water, her hair tumbling from her braids and floating around her on the surface in thick curls. Gage's fingers curled. Despite himself, he strode right into the water until he reached her. She kicked to stay at the surface, while he could still stand. Without stopping, he hooked his hands under her arms and pulled her to him, pausing for just a moment to meet her eyes – to give her a chance to say no.

When no objection came, he'd did what he'd been aching to do for days and claimed her lips in a kiss. They were salty from the water and sweet with her own essence. Gage almost moaned against her mouth, using all his willpower not to deepen the kiss. Instead he only played gently with her lips, then pulled away with a smile.

"And to what do I owe that pleasure?" Lola asked, a flush crossing her cheeks, her lips a shade pinker from his kiss. It made him crazy, how they looked like a bruised peach, and he wanted to nibble some more. Instead, he smiled down at her.

"I told you I'd kiss you if I found a mermaid today," Gage said lightly.

"You found one? Oh, you mean the drawings?" Lola pulled her lip into a pout and looked around at the water.

"No, silly. You're a mermaid if I've ever seen one," Gage said, brushing a finger across her lips. "I had to claim my kiss."

Lola delighted him with a brilliant smile before stepping closer to trail a finger down his chest. He felt every inch of him go on alert, and the world focused to a pinpoint where all he could feel was the trail of heat being left behind by her finger.

"I've been trying to ignore my attraction to you," Lola admitted, squinting up at him.

She's attracted to me! Gage bit back a grin.

"But it seems like this will be a losing battle."

"Why have you been trying to ignore it?"

"Because I didn't want this trip to be about that. I… I guess I'm looking for something more, this trip. There are some things I want to figure out."

"The Lola project," Gage said.

"Right. That." Lola looked off into the distance before coming back to him. "But you're stuck in my thoughts as well. I guess it's inevitable."

Her finger trailed lower and Gage caught it before it reached the top of his swim trunks, her intent clear. It bothered him, the way she'd said it was inevitable, as though he was just an itch to scratch. It surprised him to realize he wanted more from her. Remembering his wish, and his thoughts in the cave, he pulled her hand to his mouth, turned it, and pressed a kiss to her palm.

"Come, let's eat. I've got a picnic prepared for you."

"But…" Lola said, confusion crossing her gorgeous face, and Gage almost laughed.

"When I lie with you, Lola, it's going to be because that's the only thing you want in this world. I want you to ache for me. I've time yet to make that happen," Gage said, and brushed a kiss to her now-pouting mouth.

"Who says you'll have time with me? Maybe this was your one chance," Lola shot back. "Rejection doesn't exactly warm a woman's soul."

"I'm not rejecting you," Gage said. "But this matters."

Without another word, Lola turned and dove beneath the water. Gage let her go, recognizing a woman in a temper, and beat a retreat for the beach. Humming the whole way, he smiled as he unpacked the picnic.

It was going to be an absolute pleasure to woo the lovely Lola.

CHAPTER 16

*L*ola couldn't tell if she was embarrassed or angry, but she stayed in the water awhile, letting her emotions calm as she tried to get her bearings. It wasn't like she hadn't been rejected before – everyone had, at some point in their life. But the man had come and kissed her, hadn't he? And then to turn down what she offered? Well, he'd be damn lucky if she'd ever offer it again. Not when he had tossed it back so casually in her face.

Lola dove again, letting the water cool the heat of her face, and the niggling embarrassment that flitted beneath her mood. If she had to admit it, he was in the right. She'd moved too fast, too soon, and spoiled what could have been a very sweet and charming moment. So used to keeping men in the 'casual lovers for a few nights or a month' compartment, she'd automatically defaulted to putting Gage there. But after the moment they'd shared in the cave, and all the powerful and glorious energy she felt in this space, Lola realized she owed herself more than that as well. Sighing, she floated at the surface a moment before something glinted under the water, catching her eye. Doing her best to squint in the saltwater, Lola dove again and grasped a chain, pulling it to the surface with her.

Swimming quickly to the shore, Lola stood waist-deep in the water and examined her find. Power had all but zapped her the moment her hand had closed over it, and now all she wanted to do was hold onto this and never let go.

"Did you find some treasure?" Gage had walked back to the shore and looked at where she stood, like a fool, gaping down at the necklace in her hands.

"I... I believe I did. Oh, Gage, look!" The awkward moment forgotten, Lola bounded the rest of the way out of the water.

"Is it a necklace?" Gage asked, and Lola held it up. She was reluctant to hand it over, and Gage seemed to sense that.

"Yes, with a locket."

"What's in it?"

Etched on the outside of the large locket, almost the size of her palm, was an intricate shell design inlaid with pearl. While some corrosion tarnished the neck-lace, it wasn't bad. Lola gently opened the locket to reveal a mirror, soldered in gold, inside.

"It's a mirror locket," Gage said, looking down at the necklace. "Are there any other etchings?"

Lola flipped the locket over to reveal a crescent moon and a star etched on the back.

"A mermaid's mirror," Lola whispered, tears filling her eyes at the sense of peace that washed through her holding it.

"May I?" Gage asked, and Lola handed it over, though every ounce of her being wanted to refuse. Gage turned it over in his hand, his eyes coming to rest once more on the design on the back. "I... I know this design."

"You do?"

"It was on the pendant my mother gave me. For safe travels over water. So long as I followed the ways of the moon and the stars, I'd be safe."

"Is that... what you put on the altar?" Lola felt a tremor rush through her.

"It is," Gage said, sounding as shaken as she was. Reaching out, he held the necklace up and slid it over her neck, the long chain landing the pendant between her breasts where it nestled warmly, radiating peace and joy through her body. "It's meant for you."

"How do you know?"

"I can see it on your face. You're glowing."

"It feels... I don't know. I *feel*." Lola brought her fist to her heart.

Gage reached out and took her hand, tugging a bit as

he led her from the water to where he'd set up the picnic.

"Come, tell me what you feel."

It was the first time a man had asked her that in a long time. Pleasure swept through her and, happy that the moment after the kiss had passed, Lola resigned herself to the fact that Gage was going to be nothing more than a friend.

And for that, she was grateful. Looking at him now, with the pendant on her neck, Lola came to the startling realization that she might not survive losing this man.

Best to tread water, instead of diving too deep, Lola thought, and plopped on the picnic blanket with a smile.

CHAPTER 17

The water was choppier on the way back, but nothing that bothered Lola. They rode home in silence, both processing the beauty of the day, but no tension lingered between them. They'd had a lovely chat over their picnic, and Gage had listened without judgment when Lola explained how she felt energy from things. She'd never told anyone this, other than her mother and Sam, and she had no idea why she'd confided in Gage. But since he'd rejected her, and she'd decided to place him firmly in the friend category, Lola figured it didn't matter if he thought she was more than a little crazy.

"Thanks for a wonderful day, Gage," Lola said when he rolled to a stop in front of the Laughing Mermaid. "Truly, one for the books. I'll treasure this memory always."

"As will I... dare I say it was magical?" Gage asked

as he rounded the car and opened her door, offering his hand to help her from the car. Lola took it and ignored the thrill of pleasure that shot through her at his touch.

"That's the perfect word for it." She beamed up at him, then remembered she still needed to pay the man. Digging in her satchel, she pulled out her wallet and unfolded a wad of cash, counting off the trip fee and a generous tip. Holding it out, she smiled at him. "For you. Thank you for a great tour. Is there a website I can review your business on?"

"No, thank you," Gage said, closing her hand over the money and gently pushing it back to her. "I won't take payment for today."

"Why?" Lola asked scrunching her face up in confusion.

"Because it was nothing but pleasure. Please, keep your money."

"But it's your business. And I always pay my way."

"I always pay for the first date," Gage said, and before she could do anything, he'd brushed a light kiss on her lips, leaving them tingling and wanting more, and climbed in the truck.

"Wait. This was not a date," Lola said, turning to glare at him through the open window.

"It had all the elements of a date." Gage grinned as he shifted into gear. "Great atmosphere, great company, a lovely meal, a delicious kiss –"

"It can't be a date because you didn't even ask me on one. I hired you for a charter. Which is not a date."

"Ah, but I didn't take payment, so it's a date."

"You have to ask someone on a date for it to be a date," Lola insisted. She was tempted to throw the money through his open window, but thought it might be a tad trashy to do so.

"Fine. Want to go on a date with me, Lola?"

"No," Lola said, and turned her back, heading for the door.

"Playing hard to get. I like it," Gage said, and Lola threw up her middle finger, letting him know what she thought of him. His laugh followed her down the road, and despite herself, she grinned, too happy to care about a bit of banter with Gage.

"Well, that's what we like to see – smiling guests," Irma said from where she leaned against the door, her arms crossed over a deep blue linen sheath, her hair tumbling loose over her shoulders. Bracelets clinked at her wrists as she uncrossed her arms and stepped forward. Lola was more than certain she'd just witnessed the entire exchange, and she could only imagine what the woman's thoughts were.

"It was a beautiful charter. The Wishing Caves are seriously magickal, and it had to have been one of the most beautiful experiences I've had."

"That's wonderful…" Irma's voice trailed off as her eyes landed on the pendant still nestled between Lola's breast. A flash of shock crossed her face, followed by wonder, and then just a hint of deep yearning before Irma shuttered her eyes. But not before Lola saw all the emotions play out across her face. And in that instant, she knew.

Irma was mermaid.

Was it possible that Irma was a descendant of Irmine? A million questions leapt into Lola's mind, but she bit her tongue and waited to see if Irma could read her.

"That's… a really unique necklace. Where did you find it?"

Lola noticed she asked where she had *found* it, not bought it.

"Actually, while swimming outside the mermaid's cave today. It was in the water. It's beautiful, isn't it?"

"It is. It looks quite old. May I?" Irma asked.

"Certainly," Lola said, and slipped it from her head for Irma to examine. She watched as a brief longing flitted over Irma's face again, and she traced her hands over the front of the locket before opening it carefully. Pleasure washed over her face when she saw the mirror was still intact. Nodding once, she handed it back to Lola.

"No, I think you'll treasure this more, from living here…" Lola found herself saying, though every part of her wanted to rip the necklace from Irma's hand and drop it back on her own neck where it was meant to be. "Please, take it. A gift from me."

For a moment, Irma held the necklace, staring at it, before shaking her head and holding it out to Lola.

"It's for you, beautiful soul. But thank you for

offering it to me. Very few would. It's quite old, you know. You can tell by the craftsmanship."

"It hums with energy too," Lola said lightly, testing the waters. She was delighted when Irma's head whipped up.

"Ah, then, you feel it. That's good to hear actually. Most aren't in tune with that side of themselves. You know, from the first time Sam described you I knew I'd like you, but now I like you even more. First, for offering me this fine gift, though I know in my heart it's meant for you. And second, for not burying your gifts. Care to join me in the kitchen for a glass of wine? I've a lovely pasta sauce simmering if you'd like a bite for dinner."

"You know what? That sounds like the perfect way to end a beautiful day. I'll just run up and change and be down in a jiffy. Can I bring anything?"

"Just yourself, dear. I've more than enough to share."

Lola took a quick rinse in the glorious rainfall shower before throwing on her flowy pants and a loose tank, leaving her hair to tumble over her shoulders, and returning the locket to her neck. She found her way down the cool white hallway to the kitchen door and knocked politely.

"Come on in," Irma called, and Lola pushed through, delighted to find the kitchen as gorgeous as the rest of the house. Done in a Tuscan style, with open windows, a stone wall, and a large communal table, it was a welcoming and homey area.

Jolie and Mirra sat at the table, each with a glass of red wine. They were both as exotic and gorgeous as the day before, this time dressed in flowy silk dresses. Lola smiled her greeting at them, waiting for them to see her necklace.

"How was your tour, Lola?" Jolie said, and then her eyes sharpened as they darted to her necklace, to Irma, and then back to Mirra, who was much better at concealing her surprise.

"It was truly a perfect day," Lola said as she accepted the glass of red that Irma handed her and sat at the table. "Except you didn't tell me that Gage was the tour operator."

"Was I supposed to?" Jolie asked, raising an eyebrow at her.

"Would've helped."

"I'm not so sure about that," Jolie murmured, and Irma hissed a warning from the stove where she stirred her sauce.

"Tell us about your day," Mirra insisted.

"Yeah, we want all the naughty details," Jolie said, leaning across the table, her eyes on the locket. "That's a really great necklace."

"I found it today. In the water outside the cave. I offered it to Irma as a gift, but she politely declined."

"She did?" Jolie and Mirra said in unison.

"Oh stop, girls. You know I have more than enough

jewelry," Irma said, holding her wrists up and shaking the bracelets that clamored for attention there. "Clearly the ocean wanted Lola to have it. She feels the energy, you know."

Jeez, Lola thought, and took a big sip of her wine. Here she'd gone her whole life basically keeping her extrasensory ability a secret; now the whole island would know before the week was out, the way things were going.

"You do? That's marvelous, Lola." Mirra smiled sweetly at her, looking angelic in a misty green dress, a silver chain woven in her hair like a crown. "It's such a gift – one that too many people lose because they're so busy listening to what others tell them to feel or playing on their phones. Tell me, how do you read energy? What does it feel like for you?"

"Did you feel anything at the Wishing Caves? Did you make a wish? Do you like Gage?" Jolie asked.

"Girls, let her answer one question at time," Irma said, depositing a simple pasta plate with a lovely red sauce in front of Lola. "Go on, eat. You do not have to answer any questions from these nosy girls."

Lola took her time sampling the pasta, mainly because she knew it would annoy Jolie. She sighed over the perfection of the simple homemade ingredients blending perfectly together.

. . .

"I JUST CAME FROM ITALY. *SALUTI*!" Lola said, raising her glass to Irma.

"Thank you, dear. I'll take that as a compliment."

"Now, to answer your questions. I don't know how to explain that I read energy, other than I... feel power from things? Even inanimate objects. It's like an energy signature, so to speak. So, for example, at the beautiful mermaid etchings I saw today, I could feel the joy, the sadness, the longing, the newfound happiness from each drawing. It was really powerful." Lola held a fist to her chest. "I took some photos, it moved me so."

"Do you plan to sell them?" Jolie's voice had an edge.

"No, I don't. Those drawings are not meant for the world, but for those who visit. I just wanted to look at them again and remember how I felt there, and what I wished for. Maybe I can gain inspiration from that moment for my art. That's all. Do you think it would be okay if I showed Sam, though? I'd like to share it with at least her."

Lola took another bite and watched the women silently communicate with each other.

"We love Sam, and since she's part of the island now, I'm sure she'll be respectful of the images you share with her."

"That was my thought as well. Just so you know..." Lola looked up at them. "I'm too fascinated by the magick and beauty in this world to ever exploit it."

"Of course not; we could tell that about you right away," Mirra said, and the other women both nodded.

"You wouldn't be at my dinner table if I thought differently," Irma added.

"Thank you. And, well, for your question on Gage?" Lola almost laughed at Jolie's hopeful look. "I am attracted to him. And I think he was to me as well, since he kissed me."

The two squealed and fanned their faces.

"Give us all the details. Slowly. Leave nothing out," Jolie demanded.

Lola rolled her eyes, but couldn't stop grinning. "He strode right into the water after we left the cave and lifted me up and kissed me until I swear my toes curled."

"Ohhh," Mirra sighed.

"But, when I angled for more" – Lola shrugged, not embarrassed for wanting more – "he shut me down."

"That man did not," Mirra exclaimed.

"No way," Jolie insisted.

"Indeed he did. I'll admit, I was a little upset by it. Or maybe embarrassed? I'm not used to being rejected all that often, I'll admit." Lola sighed and sipped her wine. Irma had lit candles that created a homey ambience in the room, and Lola let the tension roll from her neck as she settled into a good meal and a nice red with new friends.

"Well, and why should you be? You're a gorgeous, well-traveled, interesting woman," Jolie said, clearly affronted on Lola's behalf. "What's wrong with that man?"

"I'll admit, I'm surprised as well," Mirra said. "I'd have thought he'd be more than pleased to have a tumble with you."

"From where I'm sitting, it sounds like the man wants more than a tumble," Irma said and raised an eyebrow at Lola.

"Ohhhhhh," Jolie and Mirra sighed in unison, and Lola rolled her eyes.

"Doubtful, Irma."

"Then why did I hear him refuse money for today and insist it was a first date?"

"Ohhhhhh." The girls again.

"It can't be a first date if I didn't get *asked* on a first date. Hiring a man for a charter boat is not exactly a first date."

"But as first dates go… what a great one! The Wishing Cave, mermaid drawings, a kiss in the water, picnic on the beach, you found a beautiful necklace…" Mirra sighed, her eyes dreamy.

"It wasn't a date," Lola insisted.

"Mark my words," Irma said. "Gage isn't stupid. He reads people very well, and despite his reputation for being a playboy, he's really not. Women come too easily to him, so they aren't a challenge. I like him because he doesn't just take, take, take, like some men who have it easy in that department. He's careful when he samples the goods, so to speak. And I think he sees something more in you, Lola."

"What if I don't have anything more to give him?" Lola asked.

"Don't you?"

"I don't know. That's kind of why I came on this trip. To find out why I've been so restless and what I've been searching for. I don't need the distraction of men while I'm on this sort-of-soul-journey of mine. I'd really like to figure out my next moves as an artist and businesswoman, not have a dalliance on the side."

"Who's to say one can't benefit the other?"

"Because lovers can be distracting, and I don't see how someone like Gage can lead me to grow on a soul level," Lola said, stabbing a piece of pasta with her fork. "Men are a dime a dozen. Different city, different man. They're fun for a while, but I'm not a commitment girl. I think it's best that I take this time to try and figure out what I want from my life."

Jolie opened her mouth, but Irma shushed her with a look. "And that's certainly your prerogative. We're here to help, or listen," she said, slanting a look at Jolie again, "as needed. This is a safe space with no judgment."

Pleased, Lola held up her wine glass in a cheers motion to the ladies. "I can see why Sam loves you so."

CHAPTER 18

*L*ola barely slept that night, and when she did, she dreamt of the sea – of diving deep, deeper than any human could go, and finding freedom in flowing through the water, uninhabited by anything. When she woke, though she was certain she'd only had a few hours of sleep, Lola felt a bit like a live wire. Her mind buzzed with all the possibilities that had opened up now that she knew mermaids were real.

She couldn't confront Irma and her daughters – Lola knew that much to be true. Just as she didn't like to share her own personal gifts with others, it would be abhorrent of her to call out Irma's secret. In her mind, a secret so large as that was life-changing, world-changing even. If society ever actually believed that mermaids were real, they'd exploit them to extinction, much as they did with the horrible captive marine shows like Sea World, or those all-inclusive resorts that kept dolphins for the amusement of humans. The acknowledgement of mermaids would be worse, and Lola could only imagine the devastation humans would wreak on the ocean in their efforts to find them.

So Lola tucked the secret away, letting the knowledge hum inside of her. She was elated to be in a space where magick was real, and let her mind wander to her art. Stretching, she rolled in bed, deliberately pushing Gage from her mind, and instead pulled a little travel notebook from her bag and wandered to her swing chair on the balcony. One of the things that had kept her up was the personal power she'd felt from the mermaid drawings the day before, and she wanted to think about how she could channel that into various forms of art. And could there be a business there? What would that look like? Lola began to jot down notes, letting her thoughts flow so she could brainstorm.

Siren Moon.

Lola stilled at that, and studied the words, turning them over in her head. Siren Moon Art & Oddities? Siren Moon Stylings? Siren Moon Gallery? She continued to kick it around in her head, making notes, playing with titles, but the general theme stuck for her. Could she create a store that celebrated the strengths to be learned from mermaids? It could be everything from vulnerability to seduction, Lola mused, her pen flying across the page. Perhaps she could choose a different theme each month. She could curate art, home goods, and local designs from artists all over the world, and have both an online and in-person store. She had enough connections that sourcing the product wouldn't be difficult – people consistently came to her for her eye for style and art – and she could be master of her own ship. Despite herself, Lola began running numbers, sketching out a loose approximation of what it might cost to find a storefront, build a website – and how would she ship her art, or would artists ship direct from their own studios?

Lola remembered what the psychic had said about bringing everything under one umbrella, and that she needed to brand herself. At the time, she hadn't understood what the psychic had meant. But now, she wondered if she had the confidence to sell herself, not only through her own personal art, but also the pieces she chose for a themed collection. Would enough people trust her instincts to support her business?

She had to try.

A joy filled her – something that had been missing for quite a while – as she began to realize that maybe this could be the answer she sought. While she'd been floating along enjoying her life for a while, it had been some time since she'd felt passionate about a project. And now, after the day she'd had yesterday? It was as though someone had turned the faucet on and it was flooding her brain with ideas.

Never one to move slowly, Lola picked up her laptop and began to search real estate listings on the island. Frustrated by the lack of information, she decided to do what she did best – have a wander-about and see what came to her.

Trusting her instincts, Lola quickly got ready for a day of exploration, slipping on a simple blue tank dress that dropped to her knees, throwing her curls up in a messy bun, and tucking the beautiful necklace inside her dress. It still hummed with energy, but seemed to have quieted now that she was wearing it. Throwing her notebook, camera, and computer in her knapsack, she grabbed an apple and went downstairs to where she'd parked her rented scooter. In moments, she was flying down the road, the wind in her hair, the palms swaying lightly in the breeze, excitement coursing through her. This could be the beginning of a whole new life for her, Lola thought. One where she had a home base she could operate out of, while also still traveling the world to meet artisans. It didn't bother her that she barely knew the island. If Sam was happy here, Lola knew she'd be happy here.

Deciding it was best to start her exploration with the locals, Lola cruised by Prince's fisherman's hut to see if he was out front.

"Hey, there's a pretty lady," Prince called from his garden, where he sat in the shade in a small folding chair.

"Good morning, Prince. How are you today?"

"I'm well as can be. Sun is shining, fish have been caught, my family is fed, a pretty lady is stopping to chat with me. What more could I want?"

"I went to the Wishing Caves yesterday," Lola said, leaning against his fence and pulling her necklace out, "and I found this in the water."

"Did you now? Come on closer, lemme get a look at this." Prince beckoned her in, and Lola swung the gate open, walking across the gravel to lean forward so he could take the locket in his hands.

"It's pretty, no?"

"Wooo, darling, it's more than pretty. You feeling that energy? That's some deep-sea mermaid energy right there, that much I know. See? You need to listen to Prince. I told you that you was mermaid, didn't I? The ocean don't give gifts like this to everyone, it sure don't." Prince rocked back in his chair, pushing his cap back on his forehead.

"I do feel it. It's meant for me. I'm not sure why, but it is. Which leads me to my next question... I'm thinking about staying. Opening a business here. Do you know anyone who has property for rent? Something I could put a gallery in, maybe?"

"Oh, pretty lady, that's even better. Helping our economy, that's a good thing, it sure is. You go on down and see Miss Maureen. She's got her ear to the ground, know what I'm saying? Tell her I sent you and that she should show you the coconut hut. It's a good spot. Trust me. The landlord will treat you nice there, but only if he approves of what you're selling."

"The coconut hut. Got it. Thank you."

"What do you want to do, pretty lady? Sell some

dresses? Your photographs? I noticed that fancy camera the other day."

"Honestly, I'm thinking I'll call it Siren Moon Gallery or something like that. I want to do a theme each quarter – art, collectibles, home styling – all based around something we can learn from the ocean or the mermaids. Perhaps the first one will be about confidence, the next about patience, then vulnerability. I'm not sure yet, but I can see where I'd like to go with it."

"Sounds perfect for here. We don't have anything like that, and now that all those fancy villas are being built, people want good art for their homes. Even better when it comes with a powerful message. You gonna be a hit."

"You think?" Lola beamed down at him and he smiled up at her, the two missing teeth making him even more endearing.

"Course I think. Prince knows," he said, tapping his head. "Now go on. Tell Miss Maureen what I said. You'll see."

"Thanks, Prince. I will."

"You pass by again soon, you hear? It always brightens up my morning chatting with pretty ladies."

On impulse, Lola bent and pressed a kiss to his cheek. Prince pretended to faint, fanning his face in delight. She chuckled and waved goodbye as she got back on her scooter and drove off to see Miss Maureen – she'd been the next stop on Lola's list anyway.

"And a good morning to you, Miss Lola. I was just

finishing up my design for you. I had a feeling you'd be passing by today," Miss Maureen called from where she sat in her rocking chair in the corner.

"Good morning to you as well. I love your bikini, by the way. It's really beautiful," Lola said, crossing the room.

"Course it is," Miss Maureen scoffed, fanning a garment out in front of her. "You think I'd make something ugly for you to wear?"

"No, ma'am, I do not. What are you making there?"

"It's a dress, a halter dress. I was thinking I'd make it a little longer, but you've got such lovely legs that I think I'll stop where I'm at."

"It's a great color. How did you achieve this effect?" Lola asked, peering at the dress. It was crocheted in a halter style, starting out pure white around the ties and then gradually transitioning through all the shades of blue of the sea to the hem.

"I just buy some of the ombre-colored material and work with it."

"Is that silver beads woven in this time? It's got a shimmer to it," Lola said, pursing her lips as she studied the way the light glinted off the dress. Miss Maureen nodded happily.

"Like a mermaid."

"It couldn't be more perfect," Lola said. If only she knew that mermaids were real, she added silently.

"Go on, try it on. Then you can tell me what you came to talk to me about." Miss Maureen handed over the delicate, soft garment and, knowing there was no arguing with the woman, Lola went to the corner of the store and pulled the curtain closed around her. Quickly divesting herself of her clothes, she slipped the dress over her head and tugged it down. The hem stopped mid-thigh, it fit her like a second skin, and Lola could only imagine how the back looked as it dipped quite low. Nevertheless, she couldn't think of a time where she'd had a garment handmade for her, so she was more than pleased to step out for Miss Maureen's critical gaze.

"Now if that dress don't get you a man, I don't know what will." Miss Maureen nodded emphatically, pleased with her work.

"What if I don't want a man?"

"Well, a woman then." Miss Maureen shrugged.

Lola threw her head back and laughed, appreciating Miss Maureen's easy acceptance of all relationships. She'd found that some islands were not as forward-thinking.

"I meant… what if I'm fine not being in a relationship?"

"Then you make the man drool, but say no. Easy."

"Fair enough. Thank you, this is truly a gift. I don't think I've ever had a dress made just for me."

"I don't do it for just anyone. But you, you're fun to dress."

"That's very kind of you," Lola called from behind the curtain as she gently took the dress off and switched back to her regular clothes. Coming out, she handed the dress to Miss Maureen for her to wrap up, and leaned against the counter as the woman worked.

"Now tell me why you come to see Miss Maureen today. What's on your mind?"

"I'm wondering if you know of any commercial real estate places for rent? I think I'd like to open a gallery of sorts here."

"Is that right? Well, wouldn't that be nice. What kind of gallery?"

"A little bit of this and that. Not just a traditional art gallery, but also jewelry, pottery, stuff for the home. From here, and all over the world. I'm still mulling it over, but it will come together for me once I see the space."

"That sounds like a lot of fun," Miss Maureen said. "Plus, I think you've the eye for it. It would be successful here."

"Thank you. I stopped to see Prince on the way here. He said to tell you to take me to see the coconut hut. Or house? Said you'd know what to do."

"I never thought I'd see the day. Well, isn't that something. Yes, yes, I see what he's thinking there. The coconut hut would be perfect. Let me get the keys and I'll show you."

"Wait, you have the keys? Is it your place? I thought I'd need to find a realtor."

"Sure, you can go on and get a realtor and they'll find you some nice spots. But we have a spot for you already, so I'm not sure why you'd go through the fuss. Come along then." Miss Maureen stood at the door, keys jangling in her hand, clearly not bothered about closing her shop mid-day to show Lola a property.

"I trust you. Oh, and I need to pay for the dress," Lola said, digging in her knapsack.

"No, it's a gift. I'd be offended. You already purchased the bikini, and you didn't ask me to make a dress. I do that for friends."

"Really? That's very sweet of you." Lola beamed at her.

"You bring me one of your art pieces sometime. I'd like that. I love adding art to my walls."

"I'd love to. I think I have a photo print with your name on it."

"I'll put it on my wall proudly. I can tell, you're a great artist."

CHAPTER 19

"*J*s this it?" Lola exclaimed, immediately smitten.

"Sure is. It's fun, isn't it? It just needs some love."

"I have all the love to give. Why hasn't this been snatched up? It looks like it's a really good location, too."

They'd left Maureen's shop and walked down a little cobblestone street peppered with colorful storefronts before turning down a small lane toward the water. There, they'd stopped in front of bright turquoise hut, with brilliant green shutters and a thatched palm roof. Just steps from the sea, it looked like the sort of spot people would pause to take photos of as they wandered past. Lola immediately imagined putting a few chairs and benches outside under the shade of the palm trees that ringed the hut, and perhaps offering coffee or wine so people could relax and browse art while also enjoying a view of the sea.

"It's an excellent location. Especially in high season – everyone strolls right past this spot," Miss Maureen said, sliding a key into the green arched door, a detail that Lola loved. There was something about an arched door, or arches in a room, that just added character to a place. Swinging the door open, Miss Maureen swept inside and busied herself unlocking the shutters and pushing them open to let the sunlight spill into the space. "Now, you'll probably want to put some screens on these windows, just to protect your art from those damn curious magpies that like to pop in and take a look. Otherwise, a good cleaning and this would shine up real nice for you."

Lola was momentarily speechless as something clicked in place inside of her. This… this was what she'd been looking for. A home of sorts, a place to call her own, a creative haven that could be a home base for her between her curating jaunts around the world.

The space was much larger than it appeared from the outside, as the hut was really more of a large cottage. With whitewashed walls, high wooden ceilings with huge bamboo fans, and a worn wood floor, the options for the space were endless.

"Now, back here you've got a bathroom and a separate room. I'd likely use this room for keeping stock, maybe a mini-fridge, your office space, and so on,"

Miss Maureen said from where she poked her head out of a back room.

"It's perfect," Lola breathed, crossing the room to see the ample space in the back room. "Could I serve coffee or wine?"

"Sure, so long as you get the permit for it. No reason not to. Let's look at that bathroom and make sure it's not in a state of disrepair."

Lola peeked her head in the bathroom. It wasn't huge, but it had all the necessary features. With a coat of paint and a pretty mirror, it would be nice enough for guests.

"Well, he's kept this up nicer than I thought. So?"

"I want it. I don't know if I can afford it, though, I'll admit. A waterfront space like this – what's the cost? Or do I even want to know?" Lola held her breath as she looked at Miss Maureen.

"Let's call him and see, shall we?"

Lola nodded, wandering the space, imagining how she'd light the one wall that was perfect for paintings, and where she'd put some low-slung tables for collectibles and art pieces in another. She knew she couldn't afford to buy it, but could she afford the rent?

"Prince says the rent is five hundred dollars a month until you get up and running, then it goes to seven-fifty. Utilities not included, and you better watch those, child – air conditioning is expensive here. Make sure you get those screens up; if the windows are open, you're likely to catch a nice breeze here." Miss Maureen chattered on, but Lola stopped her.

"Prince? This is Prince's property?" Lola thought of the fisherman in his ripped pants and faded cap.

"Don't let that man fool you with his 'I'm just a poor fisherman' act – he owns loads of property on this island. It's why he can fish all day and sit in the sunshine," Miss Maureen chuckled. "Everyone knows, if you want a good property, go to Prince."

"But… this property is prime. I mean, not only am I surprised it's not already rented out, but the rent is exceptionally low for a commercial space. I'm sure it has to cost more."

"He's particular about this property. He doesn't like just anybody in here. He's kept it empty for a while now, waiting for the right person. The money doesn't matter to him. If he likes you, he'll give you a fair deal. And that's a fair price he quoted you. Some places, I tell you, they charge double that for off the sea. You'd be foolish not to take it." Miss Maureen nodded her head sharply.

"I absolutely will take it. How do I secure the lease?"

"I'll speak to him. You come 'round end of the week and we'll have everything drawn up."

"Are you good friends with Prince? Or do you manage his properties?"

"He's my uncle! And I manage just about everything for that man, which is why I don't pay no rent at my store." Miss Maureen chuckled again. "In fact, I should be charging him for what I do for him."

"I can't... this is just amazing," Lola breathed. "Mind if I take a few photos? For inspiration?"

"You go right on and take your photos. I'll call Prince back."

"Tell him thank you for me, please."

"I will, but if you'd like, he's partial to that spiced rum they sell down at the multi-shop. I'm sure it wouldn't hurt to get him a bottle."

"Noted," Lola said. She wandered around the room, capturing photos from all angles and letting her mind run free. She turned a full circle, and stopped, beaming as she looked toward the front. From where she stood, with the door and windows thrown open, she had unobstructed views of the brilliant blue sea. To stand here, every day, and look out at that? It would be a dream come true.

"This is it," Lola said, nodding to the building. The energy was positive in the space, the breezes were nice, and the sea was at her front doorstep. "This is what I've been dreaming of. I can make this work."

"Well, sure you can. This spot is meant for you. Even I can see that," Miss Maureen said, interrupting Lola's little monologue and startling her.

"I'm glad you have faith in me. I'm going to need it."

"Even better? You have a friend to help." Miss

Maureen pointed to her chest and Lola beamed, over-come by her kindness.

"I certainly appreciate it, Miss Maureen. And may I invite you to be my first featured artist?"

Miss Maureen threw her head back and laughed, clapping her hand to her thigh.

"A featured artist! Now isn't that something? If that's the case, then I absolutely accept."

"It's a deal."

CHAPTER 20

*L*ola spent the afternoon zipping around the entire island on her scooter, taking endless photos, and stopping by Prince's to drop off a bottle of rum for the pleased fisherman. Now, she itched to get back home – back to wifi – to send photos off to her mother and see if she could get in touch with Sam.

Stopping in front of the B&B, Lola parked her scooter and jumped off, hurrying so fast toward the stairs she almost barreled over Irma.

"Oh! I'm sorry, I didn't see you there," Lola laughed, coming up short.

"No bother. Is everything okay?"

"It's amazing. And I can't wait to share with you, but I have to run upstairs first and do a few things. May I take the three of you to dinner? As a celebration? My treat."

"I'm not sure what we're celebrating, but yes, that would be lovely."

Lola bounded up the stairs and dumped her knapsack on the bed. Shooting off a quick message to her mom with pictures attached, she dialed Sam, hoping her friend had cell service wherever she was.

"Lola!" Sam gushed. "I've been dying to hear from you. I'm so mad – we've been out of cell phone range on this boat."

"I figured you didn't have service."

"You could've emailed me," Sam pouted. "How's the island? I can't believe you're there and I'm not. I'm missing out on precious Lola time. I miss you so much!"

"Well, about that…"

"What? What's going on?" Sam said, hyper-alert.

"It looks like you're not going to have to worry too much about how much time you have with me, because – well, I'm signing a lease on a shop here and I'm going to open a gallery." Lola gulped. There, she'd said it. That made it a reality.

The silence on the other end of the phone went on for so long that Lola pulled it away from her ear to look at the screen. Then a high-pitched squeal had her holding it even further away from her face. She could hear a man's voice in the background, and Sam telling him to hush, before she brought the phone closer.

"Shut up, shut up, shut *up*! Are you freaking kidding me? Please tell me this isn't some weird delayed April Fool's joke. I'll kill you if it is. Oh my god, that would be amazing. To have my best friend here? Please say yes, please say yes!"

"Yes, it's true. It's real. I'm doing it."

Another squeal. "I'll stop screaming in your ear, I promise. But this is the best news I've had in ages, I swear it is."

"I'll have to fill you in, but you know how restless I've been lately?"

"I do, yes. I thought it was just a passing mood of yours."

"So did I. But I visited a psychic in Italy with my mom."

"Naturally," Sam said, knowing Lola's proclivity for seeking out divination.

"And she put it in my head that it might be time for me to bring all my talents under one roof. So, it got me thinking and ever since I've arrived, it's just been spinning in my head what that would look like. And I think it'll just be a hodgepodge gallery and home goods space, with my stuff, local stuff, and other goods sourced from my travels. Maybe I could have some photography or painting classes a few nights a week, offer a glass of wine to visitors while they sit outside by the sea –"

"Wait. By the sea? Did you find a spot already?"

"I did. It's called the coconut hut. Just past the little downtown?"

"The blue building with the gorgeous green shutters? That's a fantastic spot. Lola, it's going to be amazing! You can even do a paint and wine night! Oh, this is perfect. I'm so happy right now I could dance." Sam laughed through the phone and Lola felt warmth rush through her at her joy. This same time last year, Sam had been broken down, defeated, and lackluster about life. On edge, overworked, and full of anxiety, she'd found her way to Siren Island on Lola's suggestion – and her entire life had changed because of that trip. To hear how carefree and happy her voice was now was a balm to Lola's soul. It was what she had wanted for her friend for so long.

"I know. I can't believe it myself. But it all feels right," Lola said. She heard Sam talking to someone before returning to the call.

"Lola, I have to run. We're getting on this sunset tour thingy. I love you and I'll see you soon. I'm so proud of you!"

"I love you too," Lola said and then Sam was gone. She hadn't gotten a chance to tell her about Gage, but there was more than enough time for that. It wasn't like things were going anywhere with him anyway, but still. Girlfriends shared such things.

Hopping in the shower, she took a quick rinse and then, on impulse, decided to wear Miss Maureen's mermaid dress. It might be a little provocative for dinner with friends, but she figured the island dress code was fairly loose. Pulling it over her head, she tied the straps around her neck and studied herself in the mirror. Miss Maureen was right, she did indeed look like a shimmery mermaid. The dress hugged her in all the right places and sparkled from the silver beads sewn amongst all the blues of the dress. The back dipped low, but when Lola turned in the mirror, it did amazing things for her, so she didn't mind. Wearing a bra was out of the question, but if she tied the straps tight enough, it looked like everything stayed in place.

Settling her power necklace – as she'd started calling it – over her head, Lola smiled at herself in the mirror. It was about as close to looking like a mermaid as she'd ever get, she thought.

"Welcome to Siren Moon Gallery," Lola whispered, and then laughed out loud. Leaving her room, she went down the steps. Not sure where Irma was, she tapped lightly on the door for the kitchen.

"Come in," Irma called, and Lola slid the door open.

"Well, well, well, don't you look yummy?" Jolie asked from where she leaned against the counter, sipping a white wine.

"Thank you. Miss Maureen made it for me. It's a little provocative, but I figured – who cares? It's pretty."

"It is indeed. And you're lucky to have her make you something. She does beautiful work," Mirra said.

"Will you both join us for dinner as well?" Lola asked.

"We'd love to. Where would you like to go?"

"Can we try out Lucas' restaurant? The one with the swings at the bar? I've heard Sam talk about it and I'd love to go."

"Perfect. I'm ready when you are," Irma said, and the girls all nodded.

"Oh…" Lola stopped short. "Should we call a taxi? I only have my scooter."

"I'll drive us. That's fine," Irma said, and they left the kitchen and piled into the truck.

"What are we celebrating?" Jolie demanded on the drive to town.

"I'll tell you over dinner. It's a surprise," Lola said, just because she liked annoying Jolie.

"Hmpf. Maybe I should have stayed home," Jolie grumbled, and Irma poked her leg.

"Don't get grumpy when people don't immediately do what you want."

"Yeah, Jolie; anyway, she's only doing it because she knows it annoys you," Mirra pointed out. Jolie swiveled to glare at Lola.

"Is that true?"

"It is," Lola grinned, unapologetic.

"I knew I liked you," Jolie said, her annoyance forgotten.

The restaurant was charming, with a great island vibe, and was quite busy. The swing chairs by the bar were a particular favorite, and Lola could understand why. They were fun and whimsical – part of the reason why she so enjoyed sitting in the one on her porch at the B&B.

Luckily, they were able to find a table and the waiter, knowing Irma, quickly brought them a pitcher of sangria. They poured their glasses, then Lola leveled a look at Jolie.

"So, I'd like to announce that I'm going to open an art gallery here," Lola said.

The women all exclaimed at once, but Lola held up her hand to shush them for a moment. "I think I'd like to call it Siren Moon Gallery. It will have everything from my personal art to local art to home goods and jewelry sourced from around the world. Sort of a hodgepodge of whatever my mood is. But I'd like to theme it a bit on mermaids, or at least the lessons they can teach us. Every few months the theme could be something like sensuality or confidence, and I would pick designs based on that. At least that's what I'm thinking. And maybe do a wine and paint night one night a week. Things like that."

"Absolutely you should. It's going to be a hit. I love the name too. Where will it be?" Irma asked, raising a glass in a cheers to Lola.

"Do you know the coconut hut?"

"Yes! That's a perfect spot. Oh, I'm so excited," Mirra exclaimed. "I bet Sam is too."

"She screamed so loud I had to hold the phone away from my ear," Lola admitted.

"Well, then, may we be the first to welcome you to Siren Island."

"Oh, that just gave me shivers." Lola laughed, clinking glasses with them. "I know this may seem impulsive. But it just feels right. I've been needing something like this, a passion project. I don't know... I just – yeah, I'm really excited."

"Did Prince give you a good deal?" Irma asked, her eyes shrewd.

"He did. He's very sweet."

"Good. I was going to give him a good talking-to if he hadn't."

Jolie's eyes grew sharp and then narrowed at something over Lola's shoulder.

"What?"

"Don't..." But Jolie trailed off when Lola turned and saw what Jolie had seen. Gage was crossing the restaurant with a stunning woman – blonde, slim, and poured into an even tighter dress than the one Lola was currently wearing. His hand at her back, he guided her into her seat and motioned for the waiter.

"Jerk," Jolie decided.

"He is not a jerk." Lola sighed, pinching her nose and annoyed at herself for being bothered by it. "Remember? We're not dating."

"He kissed you," Mirra said, her eyes soft with worry.

"So what? That isn't exactly a marriage proposal. Listen, ladies, thank you for your concern, but it's fine. Truly. I travel the world constantly, and I take lovers as I see fit. This is part of the deal. It's okay. Plus, I'm too excited about my new adventure to care much."

"And if you're not interested in anything with him, then it's best not to get involved. Though I'm pretty sure that's his work colleague. But I digress," Irma said. "Islands are essentially small towns. Everybody knows everybody else's gossip. No need to get tangled in the coconut telegraph if you don't have to."

"See? Even better. Now let's talk paint colors," Lola said, wanting to steer them away from the topic of Gage.

But it took everything in her power not to glance back over her shoulder and see what he was doing.

CHAPTER 21

"*L*adies, don't you all look lovely this evening?"

Lola almost rolled her eyes when she heard Gage's voice at their table. Deciding on restraint, she smiled up at him.

"Thank you, we most certainly do," Jolie purred.

"It isn't often that I see you out on the town. What's the occasion?" Gage asked, and Lola tried to ignore the tug of attraction she felt for him. He looked particularly good this evening in a white linen shirt, the sleeves rolled up his tanned forearms, and pressed green pants. She missed seeing the necklace at his throat, but it reminded her of where she'd last seen it.

"Lola's moving to Siren Island. She's going to open an art gallery here," Mirra said.

Gage's eyebrows rose in surprise before happiness washed over his face. "Is that true? That's fantastic news. Congratulations!" He bent to brush a kiss over her cheek and Lola flushed, his nearness doing things to her she didn't want to think about.

She smiled. "Thank you. I'm looking forward to tackling this new project."

"May I buy you all a round of drinks? To celebrate?"

"Sure…" Jolie said, then caught Irma's look.

"Actually, we're on our way out. But you can buy one for Lola," Irma said smoothly, standing from the table. The girls followed suit. "Thank you for a lovely dinner, Lola. And welcome to the island."

"Wait… but…" Lola stammered, but the ladies were already across the restaurant, Irma having neatly maneuvered Lola into having a drink with Gage.

"Looks like you're all mine," Gage laughed, winking at her and gesturing to a chair. "May I?"

Beaten, Lola could only nod.

Gage signaled for the waiter and settled in, running his gaze over Lola.

"Miss Maureen's work?"

"It is."

"You take my breath away," Gage said, heat in his eyes. For a moment Lola lost hers as well before she pulled herself back.

"Thank you. Does your date mind that you're over here flirting with me?" Lola asked, hating to sound bitchy… but thinking she likely sounded bitchy.

Gage's grin widened.

"Is that jealousy I'm sensing?"

"No," Lola sniffed, as the waiter stopped at their table. Gage looked at her. "Dark & Stormy, please."

"I'll take the same."

"She's a colleague," Gage said, reading Lola easily.

"That's quite a dress for a work meeting," Lola said, and immediately felt annoyed with herself. She sounded like a nagging girlfriend. "Listen, your business is your own. Who you date or don't date is up to you. Did it bother me a little to see you with another woman? Yes, I'll admit it because I like to think I can be honest with myself and others about my feelings."

"Tell me more about these feelings; I'm dying to know," Gage said, leaning forward with a smile on his lips.

"Oh, don't pull that whole charming thing you do on me." Lola pointed a finger at him and glared.

"I'm not pulling anything. I swear this is just me. But I really would like to know what feelings you have. And if they match mine," Gage said, dangling that little tidbit in front of her while the waiter dropped their drinks off.

"Congratulations on your new venture. I look forward to being a customer," Gage said. He tapped his glass to hers before drinking, while his brilliant green eyes held her own.

"Thank you," Lola said and then looked away, hoping they could move past his earlier question.

"So? These feelings?"

Lola sighed, playing with the bamboo straw that

came with her drink. "It's no surprise that I find you attractive. I'm not sure why we need to belabor the point."

"I'm very attracted to you as well," Gage said, his grin widening in his face.

"But it's not going anywhere. Especially now that I'm moving to the island," Lola said, leaning back and leveling a stern look at him.

"Wouldn't that be exactly the reason it *should* go somewhere?" Gage asked, confusion crossing his handsome face. "We can take time to get to know each other, see if there's something more there…"

"I… listen, I'm not great at commitments. They make me itchy. I've watched my mom get married five times in my life. I would hate to let you down, if that was the road we went down."

"Who's to say that would be our road?" Gage asked, and Lola felt a little thrill of excitement wash through her at the word *our*.

"Why would you be any different from any other guy I've dated?" Lola asked, then winced at the flash of hurt that crossed Gage's face. Reaching out, she squeezed his arm. "I'm sorry. That came out way harsher than I anticipated or intended it to be. Listen, I came here to work on some things."

"I remember. The Lola project. You deflected telling me about it the other day. Will you tell me about it now?"

"I… well, it wasn't really a clear project, if I'm

honest." Lola gave him a quick rundown of the psychic in Italy and appreciated once again how he seemed unfazed by anything related to what a lot of people would consider "woo-woo."

"And you came here. What were you hoping to accomplish while you were here?"

"I don't honestly know, but I think I've found it. I've led such a wandering lifestyle – always moving on, always setting up the next vacation – so I think the restlessness I've been feeling comes from not having any direction. It isn't that I haven't had things that I'm passionate about, because I do. And I'm not ashamed to say I'm really good at what I do."

"And what does all of that encompass?"

"I have an excellent eye for art. I curate collections well, am great at interior design, I'm an award-winning photographer, and a fairly strong painter. I'm a people person, I make connections and friends all over the world, and while many may think I'm this flighty bohemian girl, I'm actually incredibly reliable. When a client hires me for design or to find them the right piece of art, they know they can depend on me. It's vital to my reputation."

"It sounds like a wonderful life," Gage said, smiling at her. "And yet you're restless."

"I am. I think I've needed something to call my own, I'm realizing. We'll see how it goes with the gallery, but I've always done work for other people. And I'm sure I'll still do so. But now I want to do this for me – build this for me. I'm already so excited about it, I could burst. Which, to me, means that it's the right choice."

"What happens if you get restless again?"

"I think… well, the way I see it is, then I book a trip. Hire a gallery manager here who can oversee things while I'm gone, and I go get the itch out of my system – but always returning to home base. I guess, until that changes, maybe? I don't know. I'm still working it all out in my head."

"You do realize that, for someone who's scared of commitments, you're making a fairly big one, don't you?"

"I know," Lola laughed and pressed her hands to her warm cheeks. "I'm still trying to wrap my head around that as well. But don't you see? This is why… it's just… this is too much for me right now. I'm very attracted to you, Gage, but I'm worried that I'd just toss you aside once I've had my taste. And if I'm meant to live here and we're to be neighbors or friends, it's probably better that we don't go there."

"What if I don't agree with you?"

"Um." Lola looked at him in confusion. "I'm not sure you get a say."

"You've never had a guy court you before? Give you time to figure out what you want? A long slow slide into love?"

"Um," Lola repeated, lost in the way his eyes held

hers and the long liquid pull of lust that laced through her gut.

"Hmm. I do think this will be quite fun," Gage said, reaching over and grabbing her hand to kiss her palm before she could snatch it away. "I like you, Lola. I'm very attracted to you. But I know what you see when you look at me – you think I hop into bed with every woman who comes my way, just because I can schmooze the ladies."

"I don't…" Lola started to protest and then shook her head, reminding herself it was against her nature to lie. "Okay, I'll admit that's the impression you give off."

"That's fair. I understand it. Women have always been drawn to me. That makes some men act like a kid in a candy store, sampling all the goods. For me, it makes me pickier in my choices. I try to be kind to everyone, but I'm particular about whom I take to bed. Especially living on a small island – it would be easy to get a bad reputation or hurt someone's feelings. I'm not abstinent, but I'm choosy," Gage said.

Lola sighed. Why did he have to be an actual good guy when she had put her love life on pause?

"Then my apologies for the assumptions I've made. For me, I'm a bit the other way, I suppose," Lola said, figuring there was no reason to be ashamed or dishonest about her past lovers. "I travel frequently, and when the mood strikes, or I meet an interesting man, we may share some time together, and when the time to part arrives, usually it's with very little fuss. And I've been absolutely fine with that. Well, mostly. It's allowed me to lead an unencumbered life."

"I wonder if that's part of your restlessness, though." Gage took a sip from his drink. "Maybe you're actually wanting to form deeper connections."

"I…" Lola paused, tilting her head at him. "That may be so. I'll add it to the list of deep introspections I plan to cover over the next few months."

"In the meantime," Gage said, and smiled his dangerous smile, "I'll work on changing your mind about dating."

"Gage, we're not dating."

Gage looked around at the restaurant and the cocktails on the table in front of them.

"It looks like a date to me," Gage said.

"It's not. You didn't ask me on a date. You showed up at the table and plopped down. That is not a date."

"I think it might be a date. Especially because we shared history about our past partners. That's all date-talk stuff."

Lola buried her face in her hands. "I think it's time for me to leave… oh shit."

"What's wrong?"

"I just realized, Irma drove me here. Is there a taxi stand nearby?"

Gage just looked patiently at her.

"I'm not asking you for a ride home," Lola said, rolling her eyes.

"I thought you wanted to be friends?" Gage asked.

"I do."

"Well, what do you think friends do?"

"Give each other rides home." Lola sighed, and then tugged a lock of her hair again. "Gage, would you be able to give me a ride home, if it's not too far out of your way?"

"I'd be happy to, Lola. Considering I live just up the road from the Laughing Mermaid, it would be easy to drop you on my way home."

"You do?"

"I do. I have a lovely little villa on the water. You'll have to come see it sometime," Gage said. Lola shrugged a shoulder, noncommittal, making him laugh. "Where do you think you'll live?"

"I…" Lola's mind went blank. She'd been so focused on her business that she had forgotten she'd need an actual place to live. She still held an apartment back in the States, but was gone more often than she was there. "To be honest, I hadn't even considered it."

"Don't worry, friend, I'll help you," Gage said with a laugh, and motioned to the waiter for the bill.

"It's on me," Lola said, pausing his hand with hers. "I promised to buy the ladies dinner as a celebration. Let me get your drink as well."

"Thank you, Lola. Since it's our second date, I'll allow that."

Gage smiled the whole way home, while Lola remained stubbornly silent. She hopped out as quickly as she could, but he had already rounded the truck and stood in front of her.

"Thank you for the ride, Gage. That's very neighborly of you. I'm sure I'll see you soon."

"Can I take you to look at some real estate listings? I'd be happy to help," Gage asked.

"Um, no, that's okay. I need to look at my finances and figure a few things out first," Lola said. The truth was, she just needed some space from him before she climbed up his muscular body and took his mouth with her own.

"I'm here if you need me, Lola." Gage held out his card. "My cell phone number is on there. Call me anytime."

"Thanks," Lola said. She started to move past, but he stilled her with his hand. He brushed the softest of kisses – just a whisper – across her lips. Lola closed her eyes and breathed him in for a moment, before stepping back.

"Good night."

"Sweet dreams, lovely siren. I'll call on you soon."

CHAPTER 22

"Wooing me? Can you believe that man?"

"I know," Mirra sighed dreamily. Lola glared at her and she straightened. "I mean... the nerve of him. I'll be sure to shoo him away if I see him on the property."

"You will do no such thing, Mirra, you liar. You love a good romance. She'll probably give him a key to your room," Jolie laughed.

Lola slapped her palm to her forehead.

"Okay, enough about him," Mirra said. "First, we'll take you past the little bungalow our friend James is renting out. Then we'll introduce you to a few artists we like on island, though I think you really need to take a look at Jolie's jewelry." She chattered away, handily driving the truck toward town, then turning off on another unmarked dirt lane. Lola wondered how anyone found their way around when they arrived to this island – there were next to no street signs.

"Jolie, I didn't know you made jewelry. Will you show me?"

"I guess, though I don't usually tell people about it." Jolie slanted a look at Mirra, who just shrugged.

"You should. It's stunning work. All sea-based, with delicate seed pearls and intricate wiring. I couldn't be prouder of it if I made it myself."

At that, Jolie reached out and squeezed Mirra's shoulder.

"Here it is," Mirra said, pulling to a stop down a little lane that ended on a small hill. "It's just a simple bungalow, but it has two bedrooms. That will be nice for having a home office or if you have visitors."

"This looks great – is there beach access? We're so close to the sea," Lola exclaimed. She had anticipated having to find a cheaper apartment in one of the buildings downtown, not actually being able to afford her own little house.

"Come see," Mirra said, and held up the keys. The girls climbed out of the truck and wandered around the front of the sage green bungalow with tan shutters. At the front was a long porch with a hammock slung between two poles and an uninterrupted view of the sea. At the top of the hill, a little sign pointed to a path that led to the beach below them.

"Shut up. This is the view? I'll take it," Lola said immediately.

"Don't you want to see inside first?" Jolie laughed.

"Sure, but I'll take it."

The inside had everything she needed, Lola thought – high ceilings, two adequately-sized bedrooms, a spacious bathroom, and a small but well-appointed kitchen in the big main room. The wide doors slid open to allow the breeze in and she could cook dinner while looking out over the water.

"Done. Love it. I'll take it."

"It's a year lease, but I think fairly affordable for what you get." Mirra pulled out the paperwork from her tote bag, and Lola sat down at the counter, reading it completely through. Though she could be impulsive at times, she was still a smart businesswoman and never signed a contract without reading everything.

"Looks good," Lola said, signing with a flourish. "Can I give you a check or shall I send it to James?"

"He's off-island right now. We've been managing the property for him, so you can give us the check and we'll deposit it for you. Once you set up an account here you can just do a monthly bank transfer."

"I can't believe this is all happening," Lola said, striding to the porch and looking out at the wide expanse of the sea below them. "It seems so fast, but it feels so right."

"Trust that instinct," Jolie said, coming to stand by her. "You know as well as anyone, if it falls apart, then you can leave. Change it up. But, for now, give this a chance."

"I'm all in." Lola turned and grinned at them both. "And you two can be my first guests to a party. I'll host it soon, but for now, let's continue on our day."

They spent the day introducing Lola to friends and artists on the island, all of whom were incredibly welcoming and friendly. Lola was teeming with ideas by the time they pulled up to a little hut on a beach, where they each grabbed an ice-cold beer before walking down to a bench on the waterline.

"What a great day, ladies!" They clinked their beers with each other and Lola took a deep drink, the ice-cold beer cutting the heat just right. "I have so many ideas – I can't freaking wait to jump into building this gallery up."

"I like the name for it," Mirra said, staring out at the sea. "It's pretty without being tacky. Some places just… yeah, they don't hit the right note."

Lola desperately wanted to ask more about being mermaid, but instead she decided to try and navigate a different aspect of it.

"Well, the moon part really came from that story I read at the museum about Nalachi and Irmine," Lola said. She saw the sisters shoot each other a glance before she plowed on. "It said something about how Irmine could only come in on the full moon. I wonder why that was? Or if that's true for all mermaids? I was reading different myths in the books I picked up from Miss Maureen, and I couldn't find any consistency about the full moon and whether mermaids could walk the land. That part seems to vary depending on the culture and their history."

"Moon magick is powerful magick," Jolie said, twirling a long lock of dark hair around her finger. "But I suspect it depends on the tribe, and their universal agreements."

"Universal agreements?"

"Sure – each mermaid tribe agrees on certain things with the universal energy. I think it's why some can walk on land, others can't. I'm not really sure," Jolie said quickly, "but from what I understand, that all changed for Irmine and her daughters after Nalachi's death."

"Why's that?"

"I believe I read somewhere that it was because Irmine paid the ultimate sacrifice – losing her love to the ocean, a broken heart – that the bonds restricting on her movement between land and water were lifted. Everything has a price, you understand?" Mirra said softly.

"Ah – so if he had lived, would their life have been always that? Meeting for one night a month?"

"Essentially, yes," Jolie said.

"That's beautiful, and sad at the same time," Lola said carefully.

"We all have our lot in life, our own particular struggles or limitations placed on us. One isn't necessarily better or worse than the other – it's all in how you handle it," Mirra said. "Some people would say it would be horrible to only be with your lover once a month. I say it is beautiful to know a love like that, even if it is for but a brief time."

"Others might resent not being able to walk on land, and yet humans strap tanks to their back and dive into the sea incessantly," Jolie mused, and Mirra gently poked her.

Lola wondered if Jolie realized she'd referred to people as 'humans,' but decided to let it go.

"There's Gage," Jolie said.

Lola turned to see a beautiful sailboat leaving the harbor, a group of people on deck, heading toward the west end of the island. She could just make out Gage at the wheel, calling commands to his team. In moments, the sail rose, and Lola gasped.

"It's a gorgeous boat."

"Isn't it? You should do a sunset tour with him one of these days. It's really quite special. I'm sure he'd take you out on a private tour," Jolie said.

"Nope. Remember? I need to focus on me," Lola said.

"Didn't you say you wanted to hunt down the mermaids?" Mirra asked.

"I did, yes."

"Well, he's got a boat that can get you to the island I was telling you about. It's about a half-day's worth of sailing, so you need something larger than a Zodiac to get there. Ask him. I promise it's worth it."

"How do you know I'll find mermaid stuff there?"

"I don't. But I've heard tell of it. And worst-case scenario? You get a lovely boat ride and your own beach for a day. Can't be anything wrong with that, can there?"

"I suppose not. Why don't you come with?"

"No thanks – we have more guests to prepare for this weekend."

"Mmmhmm. I'm sure there's other boat operators who can take me to the island," Lola insisted, and saw the sisters exchange another one of their glances.

"Of course, but don't you want to give your friend Gage business?"

"He won't take my money, so that doesn't matter, does it?"

"Don't push her, Jolie, or she'll never spend time with him again," Mirra warned.

"Fine, but I would like to go on record as saying she's a fool," Jolie sniffed.

"Duly noted." Lola smiled and took a swig of her beer, watching as the sailboat rounded the corner of the island and faded from sight.

CHAPTER 23

*T*he next morning, Lola was all but bouncing out of her skin with nerves. Today was the day she went to sign the lease and could officially call the coconut hut her own. She'd already contacted one of the artists she'd met yesterday to commission a sign for out front.

"You ready to start your new life?" Miss Maureen called as soon as Lola walked through the door. She'd stopped by to see Prince on the way, but he hadn't been in his garden.

"I'm beyond excited," Lola admitted, bounding across the room to give the large woman a hug.

"You'll do beautiful things there, that's for sure." Miss Maureen pointed to her desk. "You have a seat and read through that there contract carefully. No need to be stupid in business."

"Yes, ma'am," Lola said and plopped down in the

little folding chair. She took her time going through the lease. It was fairly standard, as far as she could tell, and she noticed there was an option to lock in the current rate if she agreed to a five-year term.

"Hmmm," Lola said, tapping the pen on her lips. Could she stay here that long? A one-year lease was one thing, but five? But the rate he was offering was amazing.

"What's that *hmmm* about?"

"He has an option to lock in five years at the current rate. It seems stupid not to take it, but I don't think I've ever committed to anything for five years. I haven't even ever had a goldfish."

"I should tell you… now, he'll probably not be happy with me if he knows I told you this, but he likes you, so I'm going to tell you anyway. He's considering offering you a rent-to-buy option after the first year as well. It's rare for him to give up a property, but I think as he's aging, he's seeing that he'd like his buildings to go into the right hands."

Lola just shook her head, still trying to wrap her head around the idea of Prince as a savvy landlord.

"That's also an amazing option."

"I would go with the five-year option if I were you. That rent is a damn steal."

"That's the truth of it," Lola agreed, and she initialed the box, her heart skipping a beat as she did. Then with a flourish she signed the lease. "Phew, what have I done?"

"Started an amazing new career on a fantastic island?"

"Seems like it," Lola laughed.

"Here's your keys, darling. I'd go with you, but I have an appointment for my nails in just a bit. Oh… also, I wanted to show you these. Since you said you might want some of my art in your place and all." Miss Maureen opened a box on the counter and pulled out several items.

"Are these clutches? Oh, they are really beautiful. Just look at that beadwork," Lola exclaimed, marveling over the lovely purses and how they shimmered with color and joy. "I'll take them all. What do you sell them for? And why don't you sell these here?"

Miss Maureen waved that away. "Now I can't be standing right here while someone picks apart my art. You can sell them for me. Pay me after they're sold. We'll work out a price. I really do have to run now."

Lola gathered the bags and tucked them carefully into her knapsack, before dancing her way out of the shop, Miss Maureen chuckling after her. Lola breezed to her new shop on her scooter, and her heart jumped into her throat when she pulled up and found Prince standing outside.

"I stopped by to see you this morning," Lola said, parking her scooter and getting off. "I wanted to thank you for this opportunity."

"You have the right energy for this space. I don't rent to just nobody," Prince said, smiling at her and accepting the hug she offered him. "I know you'll make something beautiful out of it. Places like this, they need love. And it can't just be any old shop that goes in there. Naw, naw. It's why I've said no to so many people. It's been waiting for you, that's for sure."

"I promise to make you proud," Lola said, surprised to find tears spiking her eyes.

"That's the best you can do, then. Now, go on, open it up," Prince chuckled as Lola bounced to the door, sliding the key into the door of her very own space. Swinging it open, she stepped inside and cheered. "I love it so much."

"Let's get these shutters open and some air moving through," Prince said, walking around and popping the shutters open. "I have a screen guy coming tomorrow, by the way, if you don't mind. He's going to measure out and get some nice bug screens on the windows."

"You don't have to do that."

"Sure I do. I'm the landlord, and you can't have birds and bugs coming in while people are browsing this fine art. Now, I'd like to be the first to welcome you to this here space with a gift."

"Prince. You did not have to get me a gift." Lola put her hands on her hips. "You've already done enough."

"It's customary to give a gift. Please, let me," Prince said, and handed her a small package wrapped in simple brown paper and tied with butcher's string.

"Well, if it's customary, I accept," Lola said. She carefully unwrapped the paper to find a pile of beautiful shells, polished until they shone in the soft light that filtered through the windows. They were strung together on a knotted leather cord. "Prince, these are lovely – did you make this?"

"I DID. See, it's kind of like those spirit flags the Indians have," Prince said, and it took Lola a second to realize he meant people from India. "But it's shells for you, since it's a mermaid shop. You hang it over your door and I promise it will protect you from any bad energy entering. Here, I'll show you. I already put up the nails for you."

Tears did come this time, as Prince carefully hung his pretty spirit shells over her door, where they looked absolutely perfect.

"It's like they're meant to be there," Lola sighed, wiping her eyes. "Look what you've done. Gone and made me cry."

"Happy tears, I hope," Prince said, ducking his head, and she could tell he felt a little shy about his gift.

"The best kind of tears. Will you make me more of these? To sell? I can just see them, with a lovely card attached explaining how they're meant to keep bad energy from a home. I imagine they'd be really popular."

"Well, now, isn't that something?" Prince rocked back on his heels and laughed, pushing his cap up. "I never thought myself to be no artist."

"You are. This is really lovely. Just look how pretty it is up there."

"Sure does look nice, don't it? I'll think about it, that's kind of you to ask," Prince said, heading to the door. "But now it's time for me to go. I promised my granddaughter I'd play cards with her at lunch. Enjoy your space, Miss Lola. It's meant for you."

Lola turned a full circle in the shop, elated to be in the space by herself for a moment. She walked in circles several times before finally choosing a spot. Then she sat on the floor, her back against the wall, and began to sketch various layouts that made sense to her. So lost in her designs was she that it wasn't until someone cleared his throat that she realized she wasn't alone.

"Gage!" Lola gasped, bringing her hand to her heart. "You startled me."

"I knocked, but you were very intensely absorbed there. It sure is nice to watch you concentrate, though. You look very sexy. Did you know you nibble on your bottom lip? It makes me want to kiss the spot you're biting."

Heat shot straight through her, so sharp that she actively ached for his touch. So, naturally, she glared at him.

"That's not a very friendly thing to say."

"I thought it sounded extra-friendly, no? Compliments and everything."

"What do you want, Gage?" Lola asked, pushing a curl from her forehead.

"I wanted to stop by and see your new digs, plus I brought you lunch."

"You did?" Lola hadn't even thought of lunch, but her stomach growled loudly in response.

"See? You can't turn me down," Gage laughed, hearing her stomach. Turning, he walked across the empty space to the front door and hefted a picnic basket he'd placed at the stoop. Opening it, he pulled out a large woven blanket shot through with reds and blues and made a show of flapping it open and laying it gently on the middle of the floor. Next, he sat the basket down and began to unpack the food. Lola goggled at the spread he laid out before them.

"All that in just that little basket?"

"I'm hungry too, you know," Gage said, and offered her a can of sparkling water.

"Thank you, this is really nice of you," Lola admitted, settling onto the blanket next to him and stretching her legs out. Gage took out a plate and took the liberty of loading it for her with fruit, cheese, and a nice crispy loaf of bread.

"I thought a picnic for our third date would be nice. I so enjoyed our first picnic."

"This is not a date, Gage." Lola rolled her eyes.

"I don't know, Lola; seems pretty date-like to me. Look, I even have flowers," Gage said. He pulled out a sweet bouquet of flowers tucked in a small bottle, and put them next to her. Lola closed her eyes and let out a sigh, lecturing herself to be nice.

"Thank you for the flowers and the food. This was a very nice and friendly gesture."

"I know," Gage said, and Lola laughed at him.

"I really am excited about this. Everyone has been so nice, it's just… god, I signed a five-year lease," Lola admitted, taking a bite of the cheese. "That's a huge step for me."

"I heard you're renting James' place too. That's a great spot."

"How'd you hear that?"

"Coconut telegraph. You'll get used to it," Gage laughed.

"Yeah, I'm going to finish up my stay at the Laughing Mermaid and then move over there. I haven't even thought about shipping my stuff, or going to Immigration for residency. And here I've gone and opened a shop."

"Details. You'll figure them out. Remember, there's nothing worth doing that doesn't come with a little hard work. I'll help you with the shipping company and the immigration stuff. The key? Don't call them. Just go there and ask for what you need. They'll deal with you in person, but push you off over the phone. Oh, and don't go to any office between about noon to two in the afternoon. More or less siesta time."

"Is that a thing here?"

"Sure is. Everything moves a bit slower. No rush to get things done," Gage said, stretching his legs out as he looked around the space. "Tell me what you're thinking for in here."

"Well, I'm thinking this long wall here with no windows will be perfect for prints and art. So I'll want to get the right lighting on that wall. Plus, I'd like to paint in here, maybe an accent wall over there." Lola went on to explain all her thoughts while Gage just watched her. By the time she'd run down, she smiled sheepishly at him. "I know, I have a lot of ideas."

Gage bent, capturing her mouth with his before she could stop him. And in all honesty, she didn't really want to stop him. She had been trying to stay strong and ignore her attraction to him, but it was impossible once his lips were on hers.

He tasted like the sea.

Lola sighed against his lips and he took that as invitation to deepen the kiss, sliding his tongue past her lips for a taste, a delicate dance that pulled her in. Lola had to touch him, had to feel – she reached out, wrapping her arms around him as he pulled her into his lap to straddle him like she weighed nothing at all. Lola ran her hands up his shoulders, feeling the muscles that bunched there, as he expertly seduced her with his lips. Dying to feel his hair beneath her hands, Lola tugged the leather cord that held it back and ran her hands through his hair, loving the feel of it.

Her body moved of its own accord, her hips beginning the age-old dance as she rubbed against his hard length, moaning into his mouth as his hands trailed up her back and settled back down at her hips. Her breasts felt heavy, aching for his touch, and she arched her back in invitation. When he pulled away, both of them were breathing heavy, their eyes locked on each other's.

"Your eyes do change color," Lola said, entranced to see that the green had deepened to an almost turquoise blue.

"So do yours. You've gone almost yellow, like a cat," Gage said, lazily stroking a hand up and down her back. And like a cat, Lola wanted to arch into his hand, and beg to be stroked.

"Gage…" Lola began, but he put a finger over her lips.

"Don't say it. Just leave this moment as is. We've been having such a nice time – don't let your thoughts get in the way," Gage said, and Lola sighed, easing herself gently off of him, though her body screamed in protest.

"I just –"

"Need to trust your feelings and not try to control or label this?" Gage suggested.

"I like knowing where things stand. Murky waters worry me."

"There's nothing murky here. I've been very clear about my intention to court you."

"Court me." Lola laughed at the old-fashioned word. "And I've been very clear that I'm not open for courting."

"Those swollen lips and bedroom eyes say differently," Gage said, running a finger over her lips. She almost bit it just to prove him wrong.

"That's lust. It happens," Lola said, pulling her legs to her chest and wrapping her arms around them, feeling like a stubborn child.

"It's more than lust, but I'll let you think that for now. So, tell me, what color are you thinking about painting your accent wall?"

"You want to talk paint colors after that kiss?"

"Sure, why not? Decorating really turns me on," Gage said, and Lola laughed.

"It does not."

"Sure it does. Put on the HGTV channel and it's like porn for me."

Lola couldn't help laughing as she punched him lightly in the shoulder, amazed at how easily he navigated them past sticky moments, and yet still seemed to get exactly his way.

"Thanks for the floor picnic, Gage. This was nice."

"I wonder what date number four will look like," Gage mused as he stood and began packing the picnic.

"There is not going to be a date number four," Lola insisted, but she was speaking to his back as he left her space.

"Yes there will be," he called over his shoulder, and this time Lola did stomp her foot like a child.

But she couldn't stop smiling the rest of the day.

CHAPTER 24

*L*ola spent the next two days in a flurry of design and research, broken by constant interruptions from curious islanders. It seemed that once the word was out that a new store would be opening, everyone needed to come by and see what was happening. In some respects, it was frustrating to be interrupted so much; in others, it was very helpful – because instead of Lola having to track down contractors, they just showed up. Within a day she had workers contracted for painting, lighting install, and two potential designers for building out a small kitchenette area as well as an outdoor studio in the back. The more she'd thought about having her own studio – for painting, mosaics, and photography – the more the idea had stuck. It would be nice to lead classes there, Lola thought, eyeing the breezy back garden surrounded by palm and plumeria trees. She could even get local artists to teach their own arts there, maybe have a rotating schedule each week.

"Now, what kind of tables and cabinets are you looking for?" Prince asked. He'd stopped by every day to oversee the progress, as well as to chip in where he felt it was the landlord's duty to pay. He promised to help her with any upgrade she undertook that added value to the property.

"I don't quite know," Lola said, tapping her finger and scanning the space. "I was thinking something really natural looking, like roughhewn out of a still-visible tree or something like that."

"Hand-carved?"

"Sure, if it's done well. I want rustic, but in theme with island living."

"You want teak then. It'll hold up better in the salty air. Here, let me show you my cousin's work," Prince said, pulling a sleek iPhone from his ripped trousers. "Here, look."

"Oh my gosh," Lola breathed, scrolling the images on the phone. "Yes. Yes. Yes. These are fantastic."

The images showed tables with hand-carved bases featuring turtles, fish, and several with gorgeous mermaids. He'd left the tops rustic, sanding and polishing them to a sheen, but each had its own quirks and shapes.

"He does amazing work. He's on the next island over; you'd have to take a flight to see them."

"Hmm, how long is the flight?"

Prince waved it off. "Ah, only twenty-five minutes. It runs every hour."

"I think I'd need to see these in person. For measurements and to decide which I like. Can you put me in contact with him? I can arrange a day to pop over and see. Is there anything else I should get from that island?"

"You were talking about lighting, yeah? Which I think you mean gallery lighting for the wall paintings. But there's one artist there who makes these jellyfish lights."

"Jellyfish lights?"

"Made to look like jellyfish, but, you know, lights."

"Can you make a list for me? Then I'll maybe go over for a day or two and source what I'm looking for and arrange shipping."

"Of course. There's only so much you can get on-island. I made sure you got the good contractors. And that studio is gonna be great for the back."

"I know, right? I keep thinking about the wine and paint nights I'll host there."

"You'll get people too, I promise you that. There's not a lot of entertainment on the island, unless you go to the bar or catch a movie at the outdoor cinema. A new event like this? You'll be busy."

"I hope so."

"What's your open date, pretty lady?"

"Honestly, I'm not sure. At least two months, if not longer. I need to get my things shipped over, source some art, set up a business account here, move into my new place… it's a lot all at once."

"Don't be afraid to ask for help."

"You've already been a great help."

"Islanders help each other. We need to."

"I understand the need," Lola said. "I hear there's a holiday tomorrow, making it a long weekend. Are you doing anything?"

"I'll go to the beach with my family, like everyone else. You can come if you'd like."

"I'd love to, but I already chartered a boat trip to Little Siren Island."

"Looking for more mermaids?"

"Why not? I figured since everyone is on holiday tomorrow, I wouldn't get much done at the shop anyway."

"You have yourself a nice time then. I bet you find yourself a pretty mermaid, mark my words," Prince hummed.

"Maybe. I'm more looking for inspiration. Plus, uninhabited island? How cool is that? I might as well take advantage of the opportunity to go."

***

THE NEXT DAY, Lola pulled up to the harbor and parked

her scooter, scanning the signs to find her charter boat. Maybe it was petty of her, but she'd chosen another company instead of Gage's. Her head was still reeling from his kisses the other day, and she'd decided space was the best option. Luckily for her, it seemed Gage had felt the same, as she hadn't seen hide nor hair of him since. Did she look for him as she drove past the marina? Maybe. But spending an entire day out on the water with him might just be too much for her libido to handle. Even though Gage said he wanted to take it slow, she was well aware of his response to her – she'd felt just how much he wanted her when she'd straddled him the other day.

Lola sighed and pinched her nose. She'd promised herself no romantic entanglements, and yet here she was, ensnared.

Lola followed the sign for Blue Bay Tours, but when she came to a stop in front of the boat, it was curiously empty. Pulling out her phone, she checked the time and looked around. She was right on time, as they'd asked, and yet nobody was on the boat. Maybe they were down below, Lola thought, studying the hull, and decided to wait it out a moment. It didn't look like she could board anyway, so she'd just have to see if someone arrived soon.

Her locket hummed at her neck, and Lola knew before turning around that Gage was near.

"And isn't that a sight for sore eyes on such a lovely morning?" Gage called, and Lola turned, sighing.

"What is?"

"You, my dear. Looking all fresh, your hair wild like you just rolled from the sheets, those kissable lips frowning at me. Mmm, I am a lucky man indeed," Gage said, coming to stand before her, a wide grin on his face.

"I don't know that how I look has anything to do with your luck," Lola grumbled, reaching up to try and smooth her tangle of hair.

"But it does. Because" – Gage reached out and snagged her hand, pressing a kiss to her palm before she could snatch it back – "seeing you is like seeing a mermaid. It makes my heart sing."

The breath left her for a moment, and for once in her life, Lola was speechless. She just looked at him, help-less to do anything, as he grinned down at her.

"What am I going to do with you?" Lola finally said on an exhale.

"Oh, I have loads of ideas. In time, though. We need time," Gage said. He ran his hand up and down the strap of his backpack, and Lola couldn't help but think about his hands running up and down her back.

"Gage, there is no *we*," Lola pointed out.

"There will be," Gage promised.

"I'm sure there are many women who would be more than delighted to date you," Lola said. "Why don't you go find one of them?"

"Because they're not you."

Did the man have all the answers? Lola tried to keep

a smile off her lips, but Gage caught it, reaching out to poke her ribs.

"See, there's a smile."

"This has been lovely and all, but I have a charter to catch." Lola resorted to grumpiness again.

"Really? With what crew?" Gage looked around at the boat, still dead silent, and Lola had a sinking feeling she knew what was coming.

"I booked with Blue Bay." Lola pointed to the boat.

"Ah, she wounds me." Gage held a hand to his heart. "Here I thought we were friends and all, and you go with another charter company?"

"You won't take my money!" Lola protested.

"True, true. There is that," Gage nodded. "Unfortunately for you and lucky for me, it looks like you're stuck with me this trip anyway."

"Why?" Lola demanded.

"Because the owner of Blue Bay asked if I would take the charter, as it's a local holiday and he wants to spend it with his family. Since it was only one person, it didn't make sense for him to take the boat out. He wouldn't make a profit, just considering the cost of fuel alone."

"You aren't going to make a profit either then," Lola pointed out.

"Well, one, no, because I won't take your money. Two, I also have a sail, so I don't use fuel the whole time. And, three, I do profit because I get to spend the day with you. I call that a win-win-win."

"Why do I find your unflappable confidence annoying?" Lola asked, glaring at him. Gage threw his head back and laughed, slinging an arm over her shoulder and directing her down the dock.

"You'll get used to it," Gage promised.

"Doubtful," Lola said.

CHAPTER 25

"*I*t's a beautiful boat," Lola said, coming to stand in front of the sailboat – or was it a yacht? She wasn't entirely well-versed on all the boating terms.

"Thank you."

"*Fantasea*? Why did you name it that?"

"I think because I thought it was a whimsical name for such a drastic life change for me. But I did… fantasize about this, I guess, for the two years it took me to take my courses and grow confident enough to captain a vessel. I'd daydream about cruising to the islands while I was stuck at my desk."

"Meeting all those famous people, traveling the world," Lola said.

"There was that, and it certainly wasn't a bad thing. But my time had come to leave. I didn't have the edge anymore, nor did I really want it. I craved a simpler life, and now I have it."

"You don't get antsy?"

"At times. Then I book a vacation or get on my boat and cruise the islands for a few weeks."

"By yourself?"

"Sure. I made certain to buy a boat I could take out on my own if I wanted. You'd be surprised what you can learn about yourself when you sail alone for days on end. I never traveled too far, or put myself in too much danger, but solitude can be good for the soul."

"I never really considered it," Lola admitted, watching as he hauled boxes onto the boat. "But I suppose it might be nice to disappear from the world on a boat once in a while. I've never even done a cruise – the most I've been on is a day trip on boats. I guess I always felt like cruise ships were kind of gross and bad for the environment."

"They're horrible for the environment. They dump trash in the ocean, destroy our reefs, waste so much fuel and food. Plus, who wants to be stuck on board with five thousand other people? I don't understand the appeal."

"I certainly don't," Lola agreed as they walked down to where the little plank rested against the boat. "Permission to board, Captain?"

"Shoes off, and then, yes, you have permission to board."

Lola bent and slipped her sandals off. Today she wore over her bikini a flowy wrap skirt decorated with poppies, a striped tank, and her necklace at her throat. In her bag, she'd brought a change of clothes and some warmer layers, anticipating it would likely get much colder on the water. But for now, the heat pressed close against her skin, the breeze all but nonexistent this morning.

"Welcome to my *Fantasea*, Lola," Gage said, shooting her a cheeky grin that had Lola smiling right back at him.

"I can only imagine how often you've used that little line," Lola laughed and stepped onto the deck, the boat rocking gently below her.

"Not all that often," Gage said. "But I've pulled it out of my pocket when needed."

"I'm sure," Lola said. "Okay, so I guess this makes me your first mate. What do you need from me?"

"Can you hand me some of the boxes down the ladder? I'd like to store some stuff below." Gage moved to a little opening in the deck and then disappeared down inside. Lola looked at the mountain of gear by the ladder and wondered why he needed so much stuff for a day trip.

"That's a lot of supplies," Lola said, peering down into the darkened opening where Gage waited at the bottom.

"Some of it is supplies for the week. The container ships came in today, so I'm stocking all my water, soda, non-perishables. Plus extra fuel and a few extra things here and there. One thing I learned quickly about sailing alone is I'd rather be over-prepared than caught off-guard."

'That's smart," Lola said, and handed off the first box. Working in tandem, they quickly got through the pile and then Gage disappeared, presumably to put things away. "Can I come down? I'm curious what it looks like down there."

"Of course, come on down," Gage called, and Lola turned, backing down the ladder into the little galley kitchen. Gage efficiently stocked the cupboards and made a motion with his hand. "Go have a look around. Behind the stairs is a hallway that leads to the front of the boat – there you'll find the loo, and the main cabin. Smaller cabin's in back."

"I've never been inside a boat like this before," Lola said, turning to survey the small galley. Every inch of space was used for storage or as a place to sit or eat. "It seems to make use of the space well though."

"Not much space on the boat means you get creative with how you use it. It's kind of like having a studio apartment in New York. You hide the table under the bed, the washing machine in the kitchen closet, and so on."

"I like it," Lola decided, noting how the teak wood gleamed. "It's cozy."

"I don't mind it. I'll explain how the toilet works or you can go have a look. It's a foot pedal push."

"I'll go have a look," Lola said, noting the pile of boxes by Gage. "Unless you need help unpacking."

"Nope, I've got it. Go explore," Gage said, whistling cheerfully as he stocked his cupboards.

Lola made her way down a narrow hallway and found a small doorway to her right. Sliding it open, she peered in to see the world's smallest bathroom, along with the promised foot pedal. A sink the size of a soup bowl and a small shaving mirror completed the space.

"Sparse," Lola murmured, then continued a few steps down the hallway to where a door was open to the master cabin. She had been expecting berths of some sort, but instead there was a double bed – almost a V-shape, tucked into the head of the boat – and shelves and cupboards lining the wall on either side. A few small windows offered ventilation for light and air, and Lola was surprised to even find a small TV mounted to the wall. She could imagine cozying up in here, the boat rocking her to sleep as she snuggled in and watched a movie.

Turning, she squealed as she bumped into Gage, and his hands came out to steady her shoulders.

"Sorry, I thought you heard me come up," Gage said.

"No, jeez, you move like a panther," Lola said, her mind immediately going back to the nice bed behind her, mentally adding Gage to the daydream of snuggling in and watching a movie.

"Sorry about that; it's the bare feet. What do you

think?"

"It's neat how they use the space. I was expecting a single bed under here," Lola said, turning again to scan the room.

"They build the bed in the shape of the hull, but it gives you more room. Plus, you can lift it and store items underneath. It's actually quite nice at night. You can pop all the windows open for a cross breeze, or if you don't have any breeze at all and are really dying in here, there's a small wall-mounted air conditioner. See?" Gage pointed to a small box on the wall, which Lola eyed dubiously.

"It doesn't look like it does much."

"It cuts the heat enough that you can sleep, which is really all that matters."

"I can see why you like it on the boat. It's like its own little floating hotel," Lola said. She followed Gage as he turned and went down the hall, grateful he hadn't made a pass at her while they were by the bed. A girl only had so much willpower; a few more hours with Gage and she'd likely be tossing him on that bed herself.

"There are far more luxurious boats out there, but I wanted something that was manageable, and not too much work. Bigger isn't always better."

Lola arched an eyebrow at him and Gage threw back his head and laughed, a lock of his hair tumbling from the leather cord at his neck.

"In *some* cases, it's not," Gage amended.

"So, Captain, now what?"

"Now, we sail."

"How far is it again?"

"Should take us a couple hours to get to. It's good we're getting an early start, so we'll have much of the day. We can cruise back and watch the sunset and arrive at the marina late."

"In the dark?"

"I've sailed in the dark before," Gage said patiently. "They make these things called running lights."

"Right, right. I'm assuming the boat is outfitted with all the necessary safety equipment and radar and all that?" Lola asked.

"It is, but I'll show you where the life jackets are, as well as a small life raft if we ever run into danger."

"Perfect. Shall we get on our way then?" Lola asked, excited despite herself. While she hadn't planned to spend the day with Gage, she absolutely would be lying to herself if she pretended she didn't enjoy his company. Or watching him as he leaned over on the boat and untied some lines. The way his shorts hugged his butt had her mouth going dry.

"Are you ogling me?" Gage demanded.

"It's not my fault your butt looks good in those shorts." Lola shrugged. "I can look, can't I?"

Gage turned and deliberately bent over slowly, taking so long to untie a knot that Lola burst out laughing.

"First show's free. Next one will cost ya."

CHAPTER 26

*I*t was a little unnerving, once they'd sailed far enough away that they could no longer see land, and nothing but the deep blue ocean surrounded them. Gage seemed to be a competent captain, from what Lola could determine, and he neatly maneuvered the boat from the harbor and out to sea. They didn't put the sail up until they were far from land and were able to actually catch some ocean breezes, and the way he handled unfurling the sail and raising it brought a whole new level of respect from Lola. This was a real-deal boat, and he'd clearly taken the time to learn his way around it – unlike some men she'd seen who had a midlife crisis, picked up a new hobby, and bought all the fancy things that went with it but never bothered to learn the fundamentals.

He looked relaxed, Lola realized, and exceptionally yummy at the wheel.

She had gone down to the kitchen for a juice, and now climbed back up the ladder and came to stand by his side. "This suits you," she said.

"Thank you," Gage said, accepting the water she handed him. "I didn't know it at the time, when I first stumbled upon the boatyard. But I've felt more at peace with this decision than anything else in my life."

"What does your family think of it? Do you have family?"

"My parents are still together. They live in Vermont now and are taking a stab at making goat cheese and raising bees for honey, if you can believe that."

"Only child?"

"One sister, who has happily taken on the burden of giving my mother all the grandchildren she wants. She has one more on the way, which will make six."

"Six!" Lola exclaimed.

"I know, right? She loves being a mom. They live in Vermont too, and the kids race all over the land. They're basically outdoors no matter the season. They're happy there, which is what really matters."

"You miss them," Lola said.

"I do, but I visit at least once a year and we Skype. It's all good. They can't travel as much, but I hope to bring the lot of them down here once the new baby is a little older. Assuming she isn't pregnant again after that."

"How old are you? Unless that's rude of me to ask," Lola said, turning to look at him. It was annoying that men only got more handsome as they got older, and Gage was at that indistinguishable age between mid-thirties and late forties.

"I'm thirty-seven," Gage said with a smile.

"No kids?"

"Nope, which I am completely fine with. My sister got that gene, I think. I figured if I really wanted them, I'd have chosen a different life path."

"You can still have children living on an island, or even sailing around," Lola said.

"Sure, but having a wife and a baby on board would likely be a lot trickier than it looks. Especially when that baby starts toddling about. No thank you," Gage laughed. "What about you? Did you grow up thinking about a big dreamy wedding and two-point-five kids?"

"Nope." Lola laughed and shook her head. "Also seem to be missing that gene. And my mom had enough weddings for me to play out any dreams I had of picking out a dress, or where to get married. I got to do all that with her."

"Do you want to get married?" Gage asked, and Lola gave him the side-eye.

"Is that a proposal?"

Gage sputtered, then laughed, shaking his head as he corrected the course of the boat ever so gently.

"No, not at this moment it's not."

"I'm a little gun-shy on the whole marriage thing. I never quite understood how my mother continues to throw herself headfirst into marriages over and over.

She claims it's because love is meant to be celebrated, but to me it seems ridiculous."

"She's a romantic, then."

"She is. And I love her dearly, even if I don't always agree with her relationship choices. Like, why marry again?" Lola shrugged. "Why not just be together with her partner? The marriage part doesn't seem necessary. Especially at her age."

"She sounds fun," Gage said.

Lola looked up at him. "Really?"

"Sure. She's not afraid to love again, she likes putting on a pretty dress and having a big party. Why not? Would you prefer her alone and at home and unhappy?"

"No... I suppose I hadn't thought about it that way. Not that she would ever just sit at home; the woman travels more than I do. But, okay, I see your point."

"I'm happy to break some of your cynicism then." Gage laughed and bumped her shoulder companionably. "Want to drive?"

"I'm not cynical –" Lola paused. "Wait, you would let me drive this thing? What if I capsize us?"

"I'll be right here to make sure that doesn't happen," Gage promised.

Lola stepped forward and took the large captain's wheel, surprised at the resistance under her arm. It felt like she had total control, and if she spun the wheel, the whole thing would flip.

"Here, correct our course a bit," Gage said at her shoulder and she looked back at him.

"How do I know where we're going?"

"See that little line on the screen in front of you?" Gage pointed to the panel of instruments. "We are the little boat. You want to keep the boat on the line."

"It's like a video game," Lola said, bending over to look.

"Sure, but with real-life consequences," Gage said. "Where's your camera?"

"In my bag," Lola said, then gasped when Gage left her to go find her bag. Holy shit, she was driving a boat all by herself in the middle of the ocean with nobody around. No land, no Coast Guard, nada. She gulped, feeling a small sliver of panic work its way through her. Then she took a few deep breaths to calm herself, and realized something else.

She really liked this.

It was exhilarating, she realized, to be able to steer the boat in any direction she wanted, knowing that there were new adventures to be found in whatever direction they went. It was kind of like how she'd lived her life, but now she understood for the first time why she'd felt so restless of late.

She hadn't been at the wheel.

Instead she'd been drifting along, following any whim she had or taking any client requests she'd felt like. There was nothing wrong with that, but it wasn't as if she'd been purposeful about her existence. Siren

Moon? That was purpose, and she'd be able to direct her path and interests based on what benefitted her and her gallery first. It was an exhilarating feeling, she realized, much like driving this boat.

"Yes, I love that. You look like a cat that just got the cream," Gage decided, and she realized he'd been clicking away with her camera, capturing her moment of epiphany.

Lola jumped, and quickly glanced down at the screen to see the boat had deviated from the line. Turning the wheel sharply, she gasped as the boat responded, sending Gage almost tumbling. But he grabbed a railing and launched himself beside her, grabbing the wheel from behind and steadying the boat.

"Whoops, sorry about that," Lola said, her heart hammering in her chest. "I didn't realize how much the boat would turn. I went off the line. I'm sorry."

"No matter, it's easy to correct your course out here," Gage said, his body warm against hers as he slowly turned the wheel, "You want to be gentle though, as the steering wheel is quite responsive to touch."

Lola bit her lip, her senses heightened as he steered them back on course, and thought about what else would be responsive to his touch.

"Also, you don't want to send the captain overboard," Gage said at her ear. "Or do you?"

"I have my moments." Lola laughed and turned, surprised to find his face still there, his lips inches from hers. "But I'll do my best not to toss you in the drink."

"Or make me walk the plank?"

"Depends how bad you've been," Lola said, her eyes still caught on his lips.

"I can be very... bad," Gage said, and closed the distance so that his lips pressed hotly to hers. Lola was imprisoned there, between his arms, her back to the wheel, as he kissed her slowly and languidly, like they had all the time in the world and didn't need to steer a boat. Lola broke the kiss, then, taking a deep, shuddering breath, she dipped under his arms and stepped away from the wheel.

"I don't want to be responsible for distracting the captain," she said lightly, gesturing to the line on the screen again.

"That's a good first mate. Think you can rustle up any snacks below? We've another hour yet. Oh, and can you hit the radio? We could get some tunes out here."

"That would be nice," Lola said, staring at his back as he began to hum cheerfully, reaching down to hit a button on the dashboard. Did nothing ruffle this man's feathers? Lola felt like his kisses made her drugged, or like she'd been hit in the gut with a sledgehammer. Her body felt warm and liquid, and she was struggling to think of anything else but dragging him down to that bunk below.

He was going to drive her crazy, she decided, and that was the truth of it.

CHAPTER 27

*I*t was kind of like the movie *Castaway*, Lola thought as they approached the small island – a pristine white beach sheltered in a small cove, a few palm trees ringing the island.

"It's crazy to me that there are just these little paradise islands out here in the middle of nowhere. Who owns them? Don't people want to buy them? Can you buy them? Or would that be foolish? Getting food and water out here would probably be a nightmare, so I guess it makes sense not to own one."

"I'm sure you can find an island to buy if you're in the market and have the money," Gage said, bringing the boat close, but not all the way in. "Ready to drop anchor?"

"Sure, what do I do?"

"I'll handle this part," Gage said and went about securing the anchor.

"Now what? How do we get in? Swim?" Lola asked, shading her eyes. She loved swimming in the ocean, but they were still a good ways from the shore and she wasn't sure if there were currents or not.

"D_ID_ you really not notice the Zodiac at the stern?" Gage leaned against a railing, his grin wide.

"What… there's a boat? Oh yeah, you told me that, but I didn't see it," Lola said. She left the wheel to walk to the back of the boat where indeed, there was a little inflatable boat with a small motor. "Huh, what do you know."

"I know that I'm not swimming to shore, but you're welcome to if you like," Gage said as he began stocking his waterproof bag. "Do you want anything in here that can't get wet?"

"Yes, my camera, please. Everything else shouldn't matter. I have sunscreen, towel, loads of water, some snacks, camera…" Lola trailed off. "Do I need anything else?"

"Bring your water shoes. We don't know if we'll find caves or what, but you'll want to have them just in case. I have bug spray, a first-aid kit, and a few other things you might need too."

"You're quite the Boy Scout," Lola said, handing him her camera and slinging her pack over her shoulder.

"Being prepared is smart. Nobody ever said, 'Oh

shoot, I'm so upset there's a first aid kit here when I just sliced my hand open.'"

"Fair enough." Lola watched as he lowered the boat to the water and then led her to a little staircase. It opened to a small platform where she could hop neatly into the boat. "That's a smart set-up."

"It lets you park your boat further out; that way you don't damage the reefs or your boat."

"Smart," Lola said again, and then held onto her sun hat as Gage gunned the engine and zipped them toward the shore, the water splashing against the front of the boat. He cut the motor as they drew close, and hopped out in waist-deep water, pulling the boat until it bumped on the sand.

"My lady," Gage said, holding out a hand for Lola. She took it, stepping from the boat, her toes sinking into the sand.

"Wow," Lola breathed, turning a full circle on the beach while Gage grabbed his pack. "This is next level. I mean, what a picture-postcard of an island! Gimme my camera," Lola said, holding out her hands to Gage. He complied, handing it over so Lola could frame up round after round of shots. The pretty sand beach led to what looked to be impenetrable bush, palm trees, and nothing else. It was a bit of surreal experience to stand on the island and realize she and Gage were likely the only ones around for hours. Lola framed up a stunning shot of *Fantasea*, thinking she'd give it to Gage as a thank-you gift for bringing her here.

"Now what? Your wish is my command," Gage asked. Despite herself, Lola took a quick photo of him as well. He just looked so… natural in the environment. In fact, she'd yet to see him flustered. Maybe that would be something to put on her list, Lola thought – figure out how to fluster Gage.

"I'm not really sure. I was told this is like a mermaid hotspot, but I'm not entirely sure how one goes about finding a mermaid. Maybe we just have a wander around the island? See if we find anything? When we get too hot, have a swim?"

"Perfect. I brought masks and snorkels, so we can have a peek underwater as well."

"I don't really know what I'm looking for," Lola admitted, and then stood back when Gage pulled a machete from the Zodiac. "Um, whoa. Wait a minute."

"It's for the bush," Gage said, pointing to the tangle of jungle behind them. "If we want to go into it, we need something that will cut through it. Nothing better than a good ol' machete. Plus, I can cut open a coconut for you if you'd like."

"Now that is definitely something I have to see," Lola said and fell in step beside him. They walked in companionable silence for a while – and by silence, Lola meant *silence*. Aside from the sound of the waves on the beach or the rustle of the wind in the trees, there were no other sounds. No car horns honking, no music playing, no doors closing. It was weird to realize just how much ambient noise faded into the background of her daily life.

"Look, there's a turtle," Gage said, and pointed to the turquoise water, where indeed, a turtle had popped its head up before dropping back underwater.

"Aww, he was cute."

"What would you name him?"

"Trevor," Lola said. Gage just looked at her. "What? Trevor the Turtle. I think it works."

"Trevor it is, then," Gage smiled and they rounded the curve of the island, where the beach turned from sand to rocks. Picking their way more carefully now, they stopped to look into the tidal pools, watching crabs zip around and little fish wiggling.

"It looks like there's another cave there," Gage said, and Lola looked to where he was pointing at a small entrance in a cliff's wall. "Should we go look?"

"If we can get to it," Lola said, and stopped to tug her water shoes on. Carefully, they climbed their way over the rocks until they stood at the opening to the cave.

Her necklace hummed at her neck as they drew closer. Reaching out, she grabbed Gage's arm.

"There's something in there," Lola whispered.

"How do you know?"

"I feel it," Lola said, not bothering to explain herself. "I… just tread carefully."

"Danger?" Gage asked, automatically tucking her behind him.

"No, just... I don't know. Sadness is what I'm getting. But also joy. Just... I can't really tell."

"I'll go in first," Gage decided, pulling two dive lights from his bag.

"No, let's go in together. I feel like we need to be careful so as not to damage what's in there, not like something will harm us. Almost as though *we're* the danger here," Lola said, trying to narrow down the feeling in her gut.

"Then we'll move slow and not touch anything," Gage said, taking her hand and pulling her to his side. Together they ducked into the opening, which was just wide enough for the both of them, though they both had to stoop, Gage more so than Lola. Slowly, they half-walked, half-waddled their way deeper into the cave, until it suddenly opened into a massive cavern.

"Holy..." Gage breathed, shining his light across the room.

"Shit," Lola finished.

CHAPTER 28

"*P*earls," Lola breathed.

"Thousands of them," Gage said, wrapping his arm around her waist and pulling her in front of him so that she pressed back against his front. Neither of them moved, just stood there and shone their lights all over the mounds of pearls piled high in the cavern. There were all sizes, ranging from the teeniest tiniest seed pearl to ones the size of Lola's hand. The colors ranged from deep lustrous white all the way to a stunning opaque grey, and Lola had never wanted to take a picture of something more in her life. She'd never seen anything like it.

"I really want to take a picture of this, but I know it won't ever translate to film the way I want it to. Besides… I think it… just feels disrespectful."

"It's mermaid treasure," Gage said at her ear. "I think I'll remember this moment for the rest of my life."

"I've never seen anything so beautiful in my life... but, why... why the sadness as well? I don't understand." Lola leaned back against Gage's chest while he held her tight, and she closed her eyes and thought, going deep within to try and read what she felt.

"I agree, it does feel like there's some sorrow mixed in with the beauty here. Like a yin and a yang; the harmony of life, I suppose."

"The human condition," Lola said, opening her eyes. "Pleasure and pain, love and loss, life and death. These are souls, Gage."

"What?" Gage said, stepping back, but Lola grabbed his arms, keeping him wrapped around her. She needed to steady herself for a moment as the rush of emotion washed through her, the necklace all but buzzing at her neck.

"Remember in the myth? Irmine collects souls as pearls and keeps them, protecting them in the afterlife. These are sailors that died at her reefs, or maybe families, swimmers, island-folk. She turns them into pearls and protects them forever."

"I'll be damned," Gage whispered. "I can absolutely feel it, now that you say that. You know, I always just sort of dismissed that myth, but to be honest, it's the only explanation. There's thousands of pearls in here. No pirate would have dumped this loot here. And they aren't native to the area – look at all the different kinds and colors. Holy shit, does this mean mermaids are actually real? I mean, I guess I kind of thought they might be; actually, I always hoped they were – I wished for them, just once, to see, you know? It's silly, I know, but –"

Lola turned and pressed a finger to Gage's lips to stop his babbling.

"I'm the one on a mermaid hunt. I absolutely believe they are real. The fact that we were allowed to see this shows that they trust us to bring no harm to them, or to their treasure."

"I…" Gage just shook his head, overwhelmed. When she shined the light toward him, it glinted off the sheen of tears in his eyes.

"I know," Lola said, and reached up to kiss him softly. He wrapped his arms around her, and Lola broke the kiss, putting her head to his chest instead. Then she turned to look at the beautiful souls of those who had gone before them. It was humbling, really, to stand here amidst such universal energy and beauty.

"We should go. I feel a bit like I'm intruding on a sacred space," Gage said, and Lola agreed.

"Thank you for this gift. We'll tell not one person," Lola called out to the room. "This will stay protected, always."

When they clambered back out of the cave, the sunlight momentarily blinding them as they emerged, Lola thought she caught a flash of movement in the water. But when she looked out again, it was gone.

Picking their way down the rocks, neither of them

said a word until they reached the sandy point and turned to look back.

"It's gone," Lola gasped.

"How…" Gage said, reaching up to tear a hand through his hair, whipping his head around. "How is it gone? We were just in there, weren't we? I don't understand what's happening."

"Is it a trick of the light? I don't know," Lola said, and Gage clambered back up the rocks, standing for so long at the top, staring at the wall of the cliff, that she wondered if he'd lost his mind.

"Gage?"

"It's gone." Gage shook his head and climbed back down, snatching Lola into a tight hug. "It's gone, and I know it was just there. I know what I saw. And now it's gone and the entrance is gone and I don't know what the hell to think about anything anymore."

"There's power in this universe that we don't totally know or understand," Lola said, though even she was shaken up.

"No wonder none of the tourists that come here have ever found it."

Lola had wondered the same thing, because there *were* day charters to the island.

"She protects it. What she showed us was a gift. I wonder why?"

"Maybe because she trusts us?"

"It was a gift… something special just for us."

"But why us?"

"Maybe we both had something we needed to learn from it?" Lola mused, walking along the shoreline so that the waves splashed against her feet.

"Perhaps. Or it could be she wanted to share because she knew we would both appreciate the beauty of what she's done. Even a mermaid might want some recognition now and then."

"Or she's lonely?"

"Also possible." Gage stopped and snatched Lola up suddenly, swinging her in a huge circle before plopping her back on the ground and pressing a smacking kiss on her lips. "I can't believe it. I just really can't believe it. This is just…"

"Beyond words," Lola said, her heart fluttering in her chest. Oh, she so had wanted to remain detached from Gage, to just have some time in her life that focused on her and her alone. She needed to know she could do this all on her own.

"Hey, do you see where the sun is?" Gage said, pulling her from her thoughts.

"It's… oh. It's quite low on the horizon. How long were we in there?"

"It didn't feel like that long. Not long enough to have an entire afternoon pass us by," Gage said.

"I don't understand how that could happen," Lola said, turning in a circle to make sure they were even still on the same island. But sure enough, there was the beach with the Zodiac, and beyond it *Fantasea* still rocked gently in the water. The only weird thing was that the sun was almost at the horizon line.

"It wasn't even noon when we went in, right?" Lola whispered, and Gage reached out for her hand, pulling her close to him.

"While I think what she showed us was an incredible gift, I also feel like it's definitely time to go. There's only so much magick I can wrap my head around, if I'm going to be honest here. And time-warps freak me out. Mermaids, I'm very excited about. Messing with time? Mmmm, not so much."

"I concur. Let's go back to *Fantasea*."

Lola climbed into the Zodiac. Even though the lost time did bother her, she was still buzzing with the amazing moment they'd had in the cave. There was so much to process that she almost felt like lying down and falling asleep. It was like her mind could only absorb so much in this moment.

Gage pushed the Zodiac out and zipped them over to *Fantasea*, and Lola crawled on board while Gage dealt with the loading and securing of the boat. She walked to the bow and watched the island as sunset began. Every once in a while, she'd see a flash of silver below the surface, and she kept telling herself it was just fish. But what if…

"Should we snorkel? Get in the water? I swear I feel like there are mermaids just below the surface. Or maybe I'm just going a little mental?"

"Mmm, best not to snorkel as night comes on. I'd

prefer it if we stay safe on board. Are you ready to go? I'll set our course back."

"I… yes. Can we watch the sunset from here, or is that not safe?"

"It's likely fine, but I'm a little shaken up by that time warp, so I think we'd better just watch it from the boat. Is that okay with you?"

"No problem. I'm just going to run down and use the toilet. Is there anything you need from me?"

"Nope, I'll be a moment storing the gear and getting the boat ready to leave."

Lola clambered down the stairs and made use of the toilet, stopping to splash some water on her cheeks and stare at her face in the mirror. Her eyes looked almost manic, so bright in her face she swore they almost glowed, and her usually curly hair all but rioted around her shoulders. Her lips seemed pinker, and overall there was a radiance to her that Lola could only assume came from discovering that magick was real.

Climbing back up the ladder, she smiled at where Gage leaned over the dash, muttering to himself. Even he seemed to have picked up a sort of glow, and she felt like she was half-drunk on the possibilities of the universe.

"Damn it!" Gage swore, and it jerked Lola out of her reverie.

"What's wrong?" Lola hurried to him and touched his shoulder.

"Our entire system is down. No navigation, no

power, I can't turn the engine over. The back-up generator isn't working. Nothing. And with no wind, I can't even sail us out of here."

"Uh…" That was about the sum total of what Lola could contribute as her mind whirled.

"Just… just let me think," Gage said, and disappeared down the ladder beneath the hull. Lola paced for a bit, feeling helpless, before pulling out her camera and moving to the bow of the boat to capture some more images of the island in the perfect light of the sunset. As the sun dipped lower, she turned her camera toward it. As she looked through the viewfinder, she thought for a moment she saw something surface in the water. Snapping away, she took many photos, not bothering to look, knowing she'd have time to review the photos later.

When Gage came back up top, the look on his face told her everything. He banged around on the dash some more, his frustration growing, and Lola found herself studying him in the golden light of the sunset. It was the first time she'd seen him flustered. He cursed plenty, but never completely lost his cool. Even in his frustration, he still kept it together. She took a photo of him as he picked up what she presumed to be a battery-operated radio, and called in.

"Yes, we have enough supplies and we're safe. That's fine. I'll call if we get it up and running. Otherwise, we'll plan to see you tomorrow. Roger."

Tomorrow? Lola stood up at that and crossed to where he stood looking in confusion at the dash.

"I have no idea how this could happen."

"I do," Lola said, bumping his shoulder lightly. "She doesn't want us to leave yet."

"So she shuts down our systems? I find that hard to believe."

"Oh, but a cave full of thousands of soul pearls, which disappeared after we left it, and a time warp – that you're fine believing?"

Gage's jawline was tense, but finally he huffed out a small laugh.

"Touché."

"Will we be safe here tonight?"

"We will. There's no weather on the horizon, we're anchored securely, and we have more than enough supplies," Gage said.

"No imminent danger?"

"No. I've radioed the marina and we'll touch base in the morning. Since we aren't in immediate danger, it's foolish to send their boats out at night. We'll wait it out and they'll come for us in the morning."

"Okay. Well, then, what are you making me for dinner?" Lola asked.

"Um." Gage ran a hand through his hair, gathering his calm again, and then shot her a smile. "The best dinner you've ever had while stranded on a boat, naturally."

"Should we go back to the beach? Build a fire?"

"I'd prefer if we stay on the boat. There's already

been enough hijinks to make me nervous. I feel like I can better protect you here."

Lola's heart melted a bit at that. She was so used to taking care of herself. In fact, she preferred it that way. But... would it be so bad to let someone else take the reins for a bit? It wasn't like she could offer much assistance in this circumstance anyway. It would be a good lesson for her, letting someone else take care of her for once.

"That's very sweet of you. Whatever you think is best, of course."

"Well, since we're without power and the sun is about to set, let's dig out some of our LED lanterns, and get all our light sources together. Then we can go through the galley and see what I can whip up for dinner."

They worked quickly, Gage showing her where the lanterns were stored, and soon Lola had dispersed them across both levels of the boat, the lights casting a cheerful glow. She wondered briefly how to get to the back bedroom, as that door was locked, but instead left a lantern by the side of the door. Gage could figure it out when he went back there to sleep.

"All set?" Gage called from the galley and Lola climbed the ladder down to where he stood at the counter, busying himself with cooking dinner.

"Yes, I think I have this boat as lit up as I can. I, um, couldn't get into the back bedroom, so I just put the lantern at the door." Lola just wanted to get the sleeping arrangements out of the way, so as not to deal with any awkwardness later on.

"Thanks," Gage said. And that was that, Lola thought, assuming he knew that meant he was sleeping in that bunk.

"What are you making?"

"My specialty," Gage promised.

"Should I set the table, or do you want to eat elsewhere?"

"Let's eat up top so we can –"

They both looked toward the top as a sheet of rain slammed into the boat, and Gage jumped to the ladder, slamming the door closed.

"The lanterns!" Lola squealed.

"Waterproof. Most everything on this boat is." Gage grabbed her arm to stop her from going up top. "Tell me your camera is down here."

"It is. Thankfully. I brought my bag down once it was dark."

"Then it looks like we'll be dining in here this evening," Gage said, casting another glance up at the roof where the rain pounded.

"Are you worried about that?"

"No; there's no wind and no thunder. We'll be just fine. It makes for a cozy dinner, is all."

"Show me where the stuff to set the table is," Lola said, and Gage pointed to one of the cupboards. Soon she had everything laid out, and had even found a way to change the color of the lantern at the table, so a pretty warm light shone across the room.

"Ta-da," Gage said and turned to hand her a plate.

"This is…" Lola peered closer at the food, and then back up at him. "This is your specialty?"

"Tell me it's not the best peanut butter and jelly sandwich you've ever had and I'll know you're a liar," Gage insisted, and Lola cracked up. Her sandwich was sliced in triangles, potato chips piled in one corner, and sliced apples were neatly arranged on the other side.

"And," Gage said, turning to pull out a bottle of wine from the pantry, "your perfect wine pairing."

"Naturally," Lola chuckled. "I had no idea that Malbec paired well with peanut butter sandwiches."

"You have no idea what you've been missing," Gage said, uncorking the bottle and pouring them both a generous portion.

"I have a serious question for you," Lola asked after they had toasted their drinks.

"Okay, and I have a serious answer."

Lola leaned forward and so did Gage.

"Why did you cut this sandwich in triangles?"

Confusion crossed Gage's face for a moment before he burst out laughing.

"Because that's the way you cut a sandwich."

"Says who? You could cut in rectangles. Four squares. In thirds. Why triangles?"

"I think… just because that's how my mom made it, I guess?"

"Ah, a purist." Lola nodded.

"How do you cut yours?"

"I don't," Lola said, and Gage's mouth dropped open.

"You just… eat the whole thing? From the crust in?"

"Yup."

"Sadist."

"I know." Lola bit into her sandwich and was startled when there was a crunching. Pulling back, she looked at the inside. "Are there potato chips in here?"

"Of course."

"Hmmm." Lola took another bite, and a sip of her wine. Surprisingly, the Malbec did pair well with the sandwich. "Okay, it's an excellent sandwich."

"Say it. It's the best PB&J you've ever had."

"Well, now, let me think on that. I've had quite a few in my life." Lola scrunched up her brow and pretended to think through all her sandwiches before finally nodding. "Sure, you win the award."

Gage threw his fists in the air and cheered, making Lola laugh once more.

"Serious question." Gage leaned forward.

"Okay, shoot."

"Are you competitive?"

"Do mermaids like the water?"

"Do you know how to play cribbage?"

"Oh, you're in for it," Lola said, rubbing her hands together.

"Bring it on, my lady. You're no match for me."

Gage pulled out a cribbage board and cards after they polished off their dinner, promising he had something for dessert later. He set the board on the table. "Now, we have to play for something. What's the winner get?"

"If I win," Lola said, "I mean, *when* I win, I get the big bed."

"That's fair," Gage nodded, pursing his lips in thought. "And when I win, I get to share it with you."

"What! That's presumptuous."

"I didn't say sexy times. I said share it with you. If you can't keep your hands off me, that's your own personal problem." Gage shrugged.

"I most certainly can keep my hands off of you."

"Then I don't see what the problem is. Plus, you think you'll win anyway, so what does it matter?"

"Fine. You're going down, though."

"Game on."

CHAPTER 29

"By one point! How is that possible? I think you cheated," Lola scoffed, throwing her cards on the table.

"How could I cheat? You counted all my points. And I even showed you a point you were missing."

"I… this game is rigged. I never lose at cribbage," Lola said. They were on their second bottle of wine, so she did what any mature adult would do.

She pouted.

"Has anyone ever told you how pretty you look when you pout? I need to put that expression on your face more often," Gage mused, leaning back with his wine and smiling cheekily at her.

Lola rolled her eyes and got up in a huff to make her way to the bedroom. Eying it up, she realized that yes, there would actually be enough space for both of them to sleep. Grabbing the pillows, she made a little wall down the length of the bed like the mature woman she was, and then used the little bathroom, using her finger to brush her teeth with the small tube of toothpaste she found in the cabinet.

She pulled off her bikini top, but left her tank top and bikini bottoms on, and then crawled onto the bed. Gage came and stood at the door. When he saw the pillow wall, his lips quirked.

"I'm thinking we'll need to slide the windows open, as we have no power for the fans," Gage said, motioning to the small windows over Lola's head. "Can you flip that one open?"

Lola turned and reached for the window, then let out a whoosh of air when Gage landed on her, pulling her into a hug and tickling her sides until she finally gave in and laughed.

"Don't be grumpy you lost," Gage said against her ear, and Lola's skin tingled at his breath.

"Have I mentioned I'm a sore loser?"

"I got that impression, yes."

"I still think it was rigged."

"Thank you for not making me go out in the pouring rain to sleep in the other bunk."

"You're welcome," Lola sniffed, then turned to look up at him in the light of the lantern. The man was just so damn handsome. He was more than that, though – kind, smart, and wickedly funny.

"You can't put these pillows between us."

"Why?"

"Because they are the only two pillows. Plus, it's not too hard to storm the wall, as you can see by your current position."

"Fine. You can have the pillow," Lola grumbled, and sighed when Gage pulled her closer.

"Mmm, you fit well." His breath at her throat made her skin tingle, and heat flashed through her. Why was she resisting this? Wait, hadn't she been the one who'd made it clear that she'd enjoy a tumble with him? He was the one who had been putting her off. It all became a tangle in her mind and she just looked up at him, a question in her eyes.

"Ah, shit, I didn't think I'd be able to resist you that much longer anyway."

Rolling on top of Lola, he grabbed her wrists and pulled them over her head, surprising her so that the breath caught in her throat.

"Gage."

"I want you, Lola. I've been drawn to you since the first moment I saw you. It's more than your looks, though – that's the easy part. I love your mind, your passion for your career, your willingness to delve into your soul and figure out who you are and what you want. So many people are happy to skirt along the surface, never dipping deeper to see what's underneath. But you? You dive deep into life. You're all in. And I... I think I'm all in with you too."

"Gage... I..." Lola looked up at him, wanting him so badly it felt like her skin burned from where he touched her. "I can't promise you anything right now. It feels like too much. I'm making so many huge changes for me – adding this is another layer that scares me."

"Tell me why you're scared." Gages eyes glowed fiercely green in his face.

"I'm scared I'll screw it up, that I'll push you away. I'm so used to being independent and making my own decisions. I don't like having to rely on anyone else or even having to think of someone else before me. I'm afraid I'll be careless with your heart."

"Then don't be."

"You say it so lightly, but I'm worried."

"Then we'll take it one day at a time. Would that be something you can accept?"

"What does that even look like?"

"We don't have to plan the future. We take it as it comes and see where it goes."

"Are you... would you be okay with that?"

"If it means I get to spend time with you? Yes."

"Okay." Lola took a deep breath. "Then we do this one day at a time. No future commitments."

"What do you want... right now, in this night, Lola?" Gage's hands still held her arms down, and her entire body felt electrified.

"I want you. Everything you'll give me in this moment," Lola breathed, and Gage's mouth was on hers before she could say anything.

His kiss this time was different, hotter, as though he was branding his soul to hers, claiming her as his own.

She welcomed him, arching into his hard body as he kept her hands pinned, slowing his kiss until she all but begged for more. Her body felt overly sensitized, and she wanted his touch everywhere and all at once.

"I want..." Lola gasped against his mouth, his lips wet against her as his tongue danced with hers, pulling her deeper until her mind blanked for a moment and all she could do was feel.

"What do you want, Lola?" Gage pulled back, his eyes feverish with need.

"I want to touch you. I need to feel you under my hands."

Gage released her wrists immediately, and Lola was on him, ripping the shirt over his head and running her hands through his hair, down the muscles of his back, while pressing kisses everywhere she could. He tasted like sun and salt and sea, and she lost herself as she absorbed his very essence. Lola moaned as he pulled the tank over her head and paused to marvel at her before licking a trail of kisses down her neck to her breasts, capturing a nipple with his mouth and licking slowly and languidly like he had all the time in the world.

The rain poured outside, thundering down, and soon they were both slick with sweat, their hands everywhere except where they each wanted the other most. Lola gasped and arched her hips as Gage licked his way down her stomach, ridding her of her bikini bottoms in one movement and claiming her with his mouth. She gasped, threading her hands through his hair as he found the perfect spot and settled in to taste her like she was the dessert he'd promised earlier. Arching into his mouth, Lola threaded her hands into his hair and cried out as he shot her quickly over the edge into explosive pleasure. She sobbed out her release, writhing against his lips as he slid two fingers inside her to test her readiness.

"You taste like the sea… like a sun goddess. I'd worship at your feet any day." Gage pulled his head up, and the look on his face almost sent Lola over the edge once more. Bending forward, she kissed him, tasting herself on his lips and wanting him more than anything else she'd ever wanted.

"I want you. I need to feel you…" Lola moaned against his mouth.

"One second, darling, and I'm all yours," Gage said, and moved to his knapsack where he pulled out a condom. She raised one eyebrow at him when he turned.

"Oh? Planning this, were you?"

"Have I mentioned that I like to be prepared?"

"I can't fault you for this one," Lola laughed, and then she could think no more when he rolled back onto her and teased her with his hard length, testing her. Slowly, he slid against her, feeling her wetness, and Lola moaned, wrapping her legs around him and trying to pull him closer.

Gage paused, hovering over her for an achingly long moment, holding her gaze.

"I got my wish."

"Your wish?" Lola whispered, flashing back to the mermaid cave. "What did you wish for?"

"I wished for a mermaid. And I found mine."

Lola's heart did an odd little tumble in her chest as he slid deep inside her, deeper than anyone else had ever been, touching her in ways that nobody had before. As she desperately scrambled to keep her walls up, Gage claimed her as his own, searing her with his very being until she was spent, her body throbbing, her mind sated, and her heart happy.

They curled together, panting, wrapped in each other, neither saying a word.

A sound jerked them from the edge of sleep, and they both sat up, staring in shock at each other as a voice, otherworldly in its beauty, drifted across the water, the rain now gone.

Where the starlight kisses the sea, is where you'll find me. It won't be so long, for in your heart is my song.

CHAPTER 30

*D*ays later, Lola still shivered when she thought about the ethereal voice that had touched her to the core. It had been Gage who had stopped her from bounding up the ladder to search the moonlit water for their mermaid.

"If she wanted to be seen, she would be."

Was that what she was doing here? Lola wondered as she painted a long strip of pale peachy pink on the wall of her gallery. She stepped back, studying it. Was all of this about finally letting the world see who she was? She'd never hidden herself, Lola thought, as she picked up a can of mint green and painted another stripe down the wall. But she'd also never launched a cohesive brand that would accurately portray who she was.

"I want to be seen," Lola said out loud. She bent to pick up another sample paint can, this one in sea mist blue, and painted a sample on the wall. She'd picked up three samples from the small hardware store on the island. The options were limited, but Lola didn't mind. Having fewer options made her decision-making process easier.

The morning after their night together, most of which had not been spent sleeping, they'd finally woken to the radio buzzing with requests for their status. Gage had discovered that the "malfunction" was no longer an issue and they'd had an easy sail back to the harbor. Since then, he'd been finding ways to drop in and see her, but they'd yet to spend another night together. He was giving her space, as she'd requested, and Lola was grateful for it. If he'd come on too strong, she would likely have shied away. Instead, he'd found ways to make himself useful: helping her vet contractors, dropping off tools, stopping by with a sandwich – uncut – here and there. It was nice, Lola decided. It was almost as if their passionate night existed in another world and instead they were now learning to be friends. At the very least, Lola knew that they could live on the island together and not have tension. A part of her was scared of being with him again, if she admitted it. Their night together had been like nothing she'd ever experienced, and she worried anything after it would be a let-down. Lola wanted to keep that moment as pure and perfect in her mind as she could.

"I like the blue," Gage said, and Lola jumped, having been deep in contemplation as she studied the wall.

"Damn it, Gage. You can't sneak up on me like that," Lola said. "I swear you do it on purpose."

"I promise you I don't. Have you ever considered that you get so lost in thought, you tune out the sounds around you?" Gage smiled and held up a bag of take-out.

"You know, I've been able to find food for myself for much of my life before you came along," Lola pointed out, but she softened the words with a smile.

"Too much? That's fine. I can eat it and you watch," Gage said, putting the food down on a little bistro table she'd brought in. Settling into a chair, he stretched his long legs out in front of him and opened the bag, setting out two takeout containers. Opening one, he tucked in with a fork, watching her as he ate a mouthful of noodles.

"Is that pasta carbonara?"

"It is."

"I love Italian," Lola sighed and crossed the room and sat in the chair next to him.

"I know you do."

"How would you know that?"

"I pay attention. Plus, of all the places you've traveled, you talk about Italy a lot."

"Is that true? Interesting. I always thought Morocco was a favorite of mine."

Taking a bite of the creamy pasta, Lola sat back in her chair and studied the strips of paint on the wall, trying to decide which she liked the best in the light.

"I think you're right," she said. "The sea mist looks the best."

"It's a nice color. Light and airy, but not so boring as plain white. The peachy color isn't bad either. What about running a stripe of that along the top of the wall as an accent?"

"That's... hmm, that's not a bad idea. I could see it. Would make the accent wall more dynamic, then, wouldn't it?" Itching to see, Lola put her food down and took both cans of paint to the wall. She painted a larger swatch in the sea mist blue, then added the pale peach color as a smaller stripe, about the width of her hand, above it. Turning, she crossed the room to where Gage sat, smiling at her.

"What?"

"I love watching you. You're so full of movement and energy. Even when you're still, which isn't often, you seem to just crackle with light."

"Do I? Huh, I've never heard myself described that way before." Lola dropped into her seat and forked up more pasta, studying the wall across from them.

"How do people describe you?"

"Flighty, bohemian, hippie, sassy, pretty, weird, unusual, awkward, intimidating," Lola rattled off, her eyes still on the wall. She pointed with her fork. "You know, I like this, but I'm not sure if just a stripe. Maybe the bottom half of the wall the peachy pink, since tables will be in front of it, and the top half the pretty blue?"

The silence drew out, and she glanced at Gage.

"What?"

"That wasn't the most flattering rundown you gave of yourself." Gage's voice was quiet.

"You asked me how people describe me. You didn't ask how I describe me."

"Do people really see you that way?"

"It depends who you are talking to. The people I went to school with, who are now soccer moms living the suburban life? Yeah, I'm kind of an oddball to them. They don't get me or my life. They crave the security of being settled. And that's absolutely fine. One person's happy place is not another's. But I think because I fall outside the norm, I'm often misunderstood, or assumptions are made about me."

"Maybe they're jealous."

"Perhaps. I don't think much about it."

"And how would you describe yourself?"

"Hmm, that's a tough question. I'm extremely loyal, to a fault at times. I can be flighty, but not unreliable. I would say a world-traveling artist with a zest for life?"

"That sounds more accurate to me."

"I have a pretty healthy sense of self and my worth, Gage."

"I see that. Your confidence is what drew me in."

"And might also scare you off. I'm a very independent person."

"I can respect that."

"Yet here you are," Lola said, then winced at the hurt that flashed across his face. "I'm sorry, that was rude. Can I add sharp-spoken to the list? Sometimes I do these little jabs and I don't know why."

"If I'm stepping on your toes, please let me know." Gage rose and took his food to the trash and Lola sighed, pinching her nose. This was why she didn't want to do relationships – all those icky emotions she had to consider.

"You aren't stepping on my toes. I just have a lot on my mind. A lot of things to juggle right now."

"I can help you with that."

"You already have… you already are. Please don't think I'm ungrateful."

Gage came to stand in front of her, pulling her up so that he could circle his arms around her for a hug.

"Say, 'thank you, Gage.'"

"Thank you, Gage."

"See? Not so hard. And now, I'm out of your hair. And I'll leave you be the rest of the week if you can give me something to look forward to this weekend."

"Like what?"

"Dinner? At my place? Saturday?"

That sounded like a relationship-type date, Lola thought, but pushed the worry down.

"That would be nice. Thank you for asking."

"You're welcome." Gage pressed a kiss to her forehead and went to the door.

"Oh, Gage? What should I bring for our first date?"

"It's not our first date." Gage glared at her.

"It's the first time you've asked me."

CHAPTER 31

"*T*ell me about her."

Cynthia, Gage's assistant and one of his best friends, smiled at him from across his desk.

"Since when do you care about my love life?"

"Since it interferes with my business meetings because you're too distracted to pay attention." Cynthia crossed her beautiful legs and narrowed her stunning blue eyes at Gage. "Talk."

"You might have seen her the other night when we were at dinner? She was sitting with Irma and the girls."

"Sure, I vaguely remember. Oh, is this the woman who's opening the new gallery at the coconut hut? I've been meaning to pass by and take a look."

Gage briefly wondered if the locals would ever stop referring to Lola's gallery as the coconut hut. Things took a long time to change around here, he'd learned.

"Yes, that's the one. Her name is Lola and she's staying at the Laughing Mermaid before she moves into James' bungalow."

"That's a nice spot."

"I know. I think she'll be happy there."

"And?" Cynthia checked the slim gold watch at her wrist, ever efficient.

"And… ah, shit, Cyn, I'm head over heels for her already."

"I knew it." Cynthia slammed her hand on the desk. "And you've been holding back on me."

"It's only been a couple weeks since she arrived on-island."

"But you knew when?"

"The moment I saw her," Gage said, a smile crossing his face.

"Aww." Cynthia's gorgeous face softened. "So what's the problem?"

"Why do you assume there is a problem?"

"Because you've been mooning about all week. A man in love with no problems would not be pouting. What's going on?"

"I don't know how to play this. She's really independent. She's made it clear that she's horrible at relationships, doesn't do commitments, doesn't really believe in the happily-ever-after."

"Ah. A strong, independent, doesn't-take-any-shit kind of woman."

"Pretty much."

"I like her already."

"I figured you would. You two are a lot alike. She was jealous of you, you know, that night she saw us at dinner. That was when I knew she was more interested than she was letting on."

"Have you slept with her?"

"That is none of your business."

Cynthia just stared him down.

"Fine, yes. And it's pretty much all I can think about. I don't know that I've ever had a more magical night," Gage said, but deftly left out the actual magick that had happened that evening. He knew he and Lola would cherish it in their memories forever, but it was not for anyone else to consume or pick apart.

"Listen to you... love at first sight. Magical moments. Head over heels. I'm shocked. I honestly never thought I'd see this day with you and then, bam! Love hits you like a brick."

"I didn't say I was in love. Smitten would be a better word." Gage sat back and stared at Cynthia in shock.

"Really? Hmm, that's not what I'm hearing." Cynthia tilted her head and eyed him.

"Ah, shit. It might be. I have a lot more to learn about her. But, yes, it might well be. Something in me knew," Gage said, touching his hand to his chest. "Now what do I do about it?"

"Keep showing up for her. It sounds like she hasn't had people in her life who were reliable. What's her family like? Close friends?"

"Just her best friend Sam – you've met her. She's with Lucas now, living next door to the Laughing Mermaid?"

"Ah, yes, I remember her. She's lovely. And the family?"

"She didn't say much about Dad. But Mom is a romantic, married five times or so, I believe, and looking for next husband. Loves to be in love and thinks it's fun to get married."

"Which is why Lola's gun-shy about commitments."

"So… she seemed to get a little frustrated with me showing up at the shop with lunch today. I thought I was being nice."

"You are being nice. But sometimes strong women have trouble accepting help. You'll want to tread carefully there."

"She said she's finding herself. This is the first time she's done something like this. It's kind of like watching a flower bloom or a butterfly emerge from its cocoon. I want to be there for every step of it." Gage ran a hand through his hair.

"You can't smother her, though. If that's truly where she's at in her life, she needs to do some of this on her own. You'll need to let her understand how you can be a partner and a lover, but not necessarily a provider. Does that make sense?"

"I thought women liked being taken care of."

"Some do. But a woman like this? She'll only let

you take care of her once she knows she can do it herself."

"Why are you such a complicated bunch?" Gage griped.

Cynthia smiled a smug, cat-like smile.

"It's what makes us interesting."

CHAPTER 32

"This is amazing!"

Lola turned and dropped her pen, sprinting across the room to hug Sam.

"You're here!"

"I didn't even go home from the airport yet. Oh my god, Lola. This is fantastic! I can't even believe this is all happening. We haven't lived by each other in ages. Well, I mean, we have, but neither of us were ever home. I've been all but fast-forwarding through my vacation. Lucas kept laughing at me because I didn't even care about being on holiday – I only wanted to get back here to see you."

Lola hugged Sam tighter, tears pricking her eyes. She hadn't realized until this moment just how much she needed her to be here. It wasn't often that Lola needed approval or support from anyone, but now was one of those times.

"I'm so happy you're here," Lola said, pulling back to wipe her eyes. Sam tilted her head, looking at Lola more closely.

"Hey... Lola. What's going on? This isn't like you," Sam said, her pretty face flushed with concern.

"I... it's just been a lot at once. A lot of really big decisions. And, just things... stuff to handle. Meeting new people. New business. Shipping my stuff here. All the things at once."

"You've met someone." Sam's eyes sharpened.

"Yeah, that too," Lola sighed.

"Okay, we need wine. Do you have wine? Shoot, Lucas is still in the car. I made him wait to give us a moment. Can you come home? Or come for dinner? I need to hear everything."

"Yes. Yes, to it all," Lola said and took a deep breath, wiping her tears. "Okay, enough of that nonsense. What do you think?"

"This space is beyond. It's just... it's so perfect for you, I can't even explain."

"Knock knock," Lucas said from the door, and Lola beamed at him. She'd met him via Skype before, but never in person.

"Lucas, I'm so glad we get to meet in person," Lola said, giving him a hug and sizing up his general yumminess. Sam had done well for herself, she thought.

"We're so happy you're here – and to stay! This is cause for a celebration. Can you come for dinner?" Lucas asked, wrapping an arm around Sam's waist. Lola stepped back and looked at the two of them, a unit, and felt tears fill her eyes again.

"Yes. She's coming for dinner. Now," Sam said, stepping forward and grabbing Lola's arm.

"No, no… those were happy tears. You look so good together. I'm just so happy for you both."

Lucas kissed the top of Sam's head. "As am I. I lucked out with this one."

"We both lucked out." Sam grinned up at him.

"Awwwww," Lola sighed. "Okay, enough shmoopy stuff. Let me quickly show you around and then I'll close up for the day and come over for dinner. How about this: Since you just got home, I can pick up some pizza and bring it over? Keep it easy."

"Works for me," Lucas said. "We just have to stop to pick up Pipin on the way home."

An hour later they were cozied up at Lucas and Sam's gorgeous villa, with Pipin torn between begging for a bite of pizza and racing around the sand in delight that they were home. The sun dipped toward the horizon, and Lola leaned back, rubbing her belly in contentment.

"This is a damn good pizza," Lola said.

"You wouldn't think it," Sam agreed, tucking her feet beneath her and leaning into Lucas on the outdoor couch. "It looks like such a little run-down shack, and yet the most mouthwatering food comes out of it."

"Just goes to show you can't always take things by

their appearances," Lucas said, his hand idly running up and down Sam's arm.

"How do you like staying at the Laughing Mermaid? I'm kind of bummed you won't be next door," Sam pouted.

"She's going to be like literally two minutes away," Lucas said. "A month ago she was across the world."

"I don't want your logic right now," Sam grumbled, and he kissed her nose.

"I love the B&B. Irma and the girls have been fantastic, and have gone above and beyond in welcoming me to the island." Lola paused, wondering how much Sam knew about them, and decided against saying anything more.

"They're the best. Don't let Jolie put you off. You just have to give her what she dishes out."

"Nah, Jolie and I are cool. We're very likeminded," Lola said with a laugh, eying up another piece of the artichoke, pepper, and sausage pizza. Pipin came and stood next to her, looking between her and the pizza she was eyeing up. "I know, buddy. I'm thinking the same thing as you."

"He's had more than enough treats," Lucas cautioned. "No more tonight."

Seeming to understand Lucas's tone, the dog walked away, settling into the sand with a little sigh.

"Oh no, you've upset him," Lola laughed.

"It's all an act. He's a con artist if I've ever met one," Lucas said. "Just look at him."

Pipin stared woefully at them all for a moment but, unable to hold it, jumped up and wagged his tail. Then, with his tongue lolling out of his smiling mouth, he did another ecstatic loop of the beach.

"See? Con artist."

"He does it quite well, I'll admit," Lola laughed.

"Okay, we've heard about Siren Moon – which sounds amazing; the concept is perfect for the island, perfect for you, and perfect for me because I'll come help you out when you're too busy. Now… is there a perfect man too?"

Lola paused for a moment. Was Gage perfect? On paper, maybe. But he was still human and had flaws. She just hadn't found that many of them yet. But they were there. She remembered him cursing on the boat when things didn't go according to his plan. Which, actually, made him that much more likeable.

"Lola? Earth to Lola?" Sam snapped her fingers and then raised an eyebrow at her. "I don't think I've ever seen that look on your face before about a man."

"What look?" Lola narrowed her eyes.

"Smitten, that's what." Sam narrowed her eyes right back.

"Am not."

"Are too."

"Not."

"Ladies." Lucas laughed and held up his hand. "Who is this man?"

"His name is Gage. He runs the –"

"Gage!" Sam exclaimed. "Oh, why didn't I think of him? He's perfect for you."

"You know him?"

"Of course. It's not a big island. Gage is a great guy," Lucas said, toasting her with his wine glass. "You have excellent taste."

"He's really delicious-looking too," Sam said, then laughed when Lucas slanted her a look. "Not better than you, baby. Just different. Still yummy. Wouldn't he and Lola make a beautiful couple?"

"Well, I don't know about that. You know I'm not big on relationships," Lola said.

Sam's face fell. "But… can't you at least try? I mean, you're staying in one place for the first time in your life. Wouldn't this be the right time to also try a relationship? You've been able to use the excuse of traveling to end all your other relationships. But now you can't. So what gives?"

Lucas cleared his throat and made a move to stand.

"I don't want to intrude on anything."

"No, it's fine. If Sam loves you, so do I. Which means you'll get to know my ugly bits too," Lola said, taking a long sip of wine as she thought over what Sam had said. It stung a bit, but she knew Sam was coming from a place of love. In fact, she was one of the few people in the world that Lola would let question her like that.

"Here's the deal. I'm really attracted to him. And I like him. As a person, not just for his body."

"It's always nice when women don't just treat us like a piece of meat," Lucas agreed.

"You like it when –" Sam said, and Lola shot up her hand.

"Okay, okay, anyway... But I also came here because I needed to figure some things out on my own. Without the distraction of a lover or a relationship. And yet, right away, I find myself falling in with a guy, at the same time I'm making all these huge decisions with my life. Everything just seems murky to me and I need to get really clear on my stuff first."

"That's fair, I guess." Sam pouted a bit.

"The right partner should help you grow into the person you want to be. Not smother that," Lucas pointed out.

Lola stared at him for so long that a worried look crossed his face, and he looked between the two of them.

"What? Did I say something wrong?"

"Nope. Lola's just shocked because she's never considered the fact that she could have an equal partner."

"Oh, well, then. Give it a go." Lucas shot her a thumbs up.

"'Give it a go' indeed."

CHAPTER 33

$\mathcal{L}$ola arrived for dinner the next night, carefully following Gage's directions to discover that he really didn't live far from the Laughing Mermaid. She likely could have walked, Lola thought as she parked her scooter and retrieved her bag with the nice bottle of wine she'd picked up for tonight.

She'd had a hell of a day. Two of her contractors hadn't shown up, which had basically stalled all her projects at the gallery because she couldn't proceed with the stuff she could do on her own until the more permanent fixtures had been installed. Her landlord back home was refusing to allow a moving company to come in and pack her stuff for her, claiming some sort of nonsense liability issue, and she'd just realized that she'd need to buy a car. While her savings account was still healthy, Lola detested digging too deeply into it, and now it seemed like she'd have to take quite a chunk out of it to accomplish all the things she wanted.

It made her a little tetchy, she realized, to have to dip into her account. Though what she was saving for, she did not know. It had just always been there, her ticket to freedom – a plane ride to another country, a medical expense paid, and so on. Now, relying on it to build her dream was scary, because once it was gone... well, she'd be stuck.

And Lola didn't like feeling stuck.

"Hi," Gage said, leaning against the door as Lola all but stomped up, brandishing the bottle of wine. "Rough day?"

"A bit," Lola admitted, shrugging a shoulder. At least she'd had time to shower and tug a pretty dress over her head before she had to get back out the door.

"Need a hug?" Gage asked.

"No, I'm fine," Lola brushed him off, starting to walk forward, but then realized it wasn't really a question when she found herself in Gage's arms. She let him hold her for a moment, the warmth of the hug flooding her whole body, the muscles in her shoulders relaxing incrementally. The necklace hummed at her neck – happy, she presumed. Still, Lola pulled away.

"Thanks," Lola said, and stepped past Gage, trying to calm the crankiness that roiled in her stomach. Pausing, she looked around Gage's home. The front door opened to a wide-open space done up in deep woods, with splashes of palm leaf prints on the furniture, and lovely underwater photography on the walls. At the heart of it all was an entire wall of tall glass doors, currently pushed open to the wide deck that wrapped the villa, the stunning blue sea just beyond it. It was earthy and beachy and just… right. Lola sighed. "What a great space. Kudos to you, because not all guys know how to use their space well. Okay, that's not fair, I'm being sexist. Let's just say not all people know how to decorate."

"I had some help," Gage said, coming up to rub her shoulders with his strong hands. "Will you tell me what's wrong?"

"Nothing's wrong. I'm just a little tired," Lola said, fudging a bit about her mood. She had no intention of dumping her problems in his lap.

"Then may I offer you a drink? We can sit and watch the sun go down."

"Thanks, I'd like that," Lola said, walking toward the long concrete style countertop in the kitchen, sniffing the air as she went. "Something smells delicious."

"I was in the mood for some Cajun. Do you like spicy?"

"I do."

"You're in for a treat then. I learned how to make this gumbo from an old shrimp boat captain I met down the way on my boat. He didn't share his recipe with just anyone, so don't even think about asking for it."

Despite her mood, Lola's lips quirked on a smile. "If I like it, I'll figure out a way to get it out of you."

"I'm sure you can persuade me one way or the other," Gage said, sending her a look filled with so much heat that she thought his spicy gumbo would likely pale in comparison.

"Ah, that's useful knowledge to have." Lola pursed her lips as he opened the wine and poured them both a glass. "Will break under sexual torture."

Gage sloshed some wine over the side of the glass and glared at her, causing Lola to chuckle.

"I'm listening," Gage said, and she laughed again.

"I can't tell you or you'd come up with a strategy to block my attempts at getting your recipe."

"No, really, I feel like you should tell me. In great detail," Gage insisted, and slid a glass of wine across the counter to her. "Have I told you how pretty you look tonight?"

"You have not," Lola said, taking a sip from her glass and eyeing him carefully over the rim.

"You look like a mermaid, washed ashore, a little bit tumultuous, your hair wild, your mood on edge, and I want you more than I can think right now." His green eyes deepened in color as he looked at her.

Lola took a deep breath, steadying herself against the wave of lust that washed through her.

"What are you going to do about that then?" Lola asked, raising her chin on a challenge.

"Take what's offered," Gage said, setting his glass

down, his fingers white as he gripped the counter tightly.

"It's offered," Lola said, and gasped when Gage lifted her from the chair, throwing her over his shoulder and bounding down a hallway from the kitchen.

"Gage! Your gumbo!"

"It's on simmer, it can wait. This cannot." Gage turned and bit her bum so hard that she squealed against his back, and reached out to pinch his, since it was so close.

"You'll pay for that," Gage warned.

"So will you," Lola promised, giggling as Gage dropped her on the bed.

There was no time for slow seduction, and neither of them wanted that. Almost desperate, they tore their clothes off, tossing them over their heads as if they were entering a battle ring, and pounced on each other. Rolling over on the mattress, Gage pinned Lola and kissed her senseless until she pushed her leg between his, forcing him to flip, and climbed on top, riding them both into sweet oblivion.

When it was over, Lola rolled off, gasping for breath as she lay on his bed and looked at his sky-blue ceiling.

"I like your ceiling."

"Thank you. I like your style," Gage said, turning to prop his head on his hand and run the other hand down her body, making her want to purr like a kitten.

"That was a bit... fast and furious?"

"It was perfect," Gage said, then laughed as her

stomach rumbled. "And that's my cue to feed you. Want a quick rinse? The shower's just that way."

"I do, thank you."

"Great, we can share," Gage said, and followed her into the large shower, laughing as she tried to push him out. Pushing her against the wall, he kissed her deeply, reaching one hand behind him to turn the spray on.

After a decidedly longer rinse-off than she had expected, Lola was finally perched back at the counter, the sun having already said goodbye to the sky, and was enjoying her glass of wine.

"You seem much more relaxed now," Gage said, as he plated their food and led them to the outside table where he'd lit candles in pretty little lanterns that protected the flames from the wind.

"I am, thank you," Lola agreed, easing back into the chair across from him and clinking her glass against his. Digging in, she moaned against the flavors of the gumbo.

"Good?"

"Oh… you're definitely getting tied up for this recipe."

Lola laughed as Gage choked on his wine, coughing a bit as he bumped his chest with his fist.

"I… think I'll look forward to that?"

"Maybe." Lola laughed at the look on his face, caught somewhere between fear and lust.

"So, tell me about your day," Gage said, spooning up more gumbo and watching her carefully.

Lola sighed and then sat back, filling him in on all the things that had gone wrong that day. Gage listened, not saying a word, and at the end of it she did feel better for having someone to talk to about it. Maybe this was what Lucas meant about having an equal partner.

"I'm so sorry, that does sound like a rough day. You know, I can call my buddy Tomas tomorrow, he'll get in with his crew and fix up the gallery in no time. He owes me a favor anyway," Gage said, leaning back to tap his finger against his mouth, not noticing when Lola opened her own mouth to try to speak. "And I know an attorney who lives stateside. I'll get him to check on that liability issue with your landlord. That's beyond ridiculous that you can't have a moving company come in and pack your stuff. People do that all the time. In fact, they'll probably be more careful with your stuff because they don't want to get in trouble for breaking anything. Oh! And I know a guy who is selling a Jeep. He hasn't listed it yet. He rents cars on-island, and after a year or so of use, he'll get new ones – tourists always want flashy new ones – so it's only a year old. But I'll get him down on the price. Maybe take him and his family out for a day of sailing to sweeten the deal."

Gage finally stopped talking and realized that Lola was looking at him with anything but joy. It took a moment for her to get words out, as the anger that had at first simmered was now threatening to boil over.

"You, you, you –" Lola sputtered.

"What?" Gage asked.

"I don't need you to do anything for me, Gage."
Screw it, the anger was boiling over. Lola stood up and
threw her napkin on the table. Turning, she strode across
the room and gathered her purse, only stopping when
Gage grabbed her arm.

"Lola, wait. What's wrong? What did I do?"

"Did I ask you to fix anything for me? I don't need
you swooping in and playing knight in shining armor,
Gage. I've lived my life very successfully on my own,
and I can handle my problems on my own," Lola
seethed. "I am not some wilting damsel in distress who
can't figure out how to handle her own problems. I
never have been. I don't need you, or anyone else,
coming in and fixing my issues. They are my problems
and I will handle them as I see fit."

"Lola… I was just trying to help," Gage said, his
eyes wounded.

"Don't you understand? I don't need your help. I
need to do this on my own. I've told you that all along,
but you just don't listen, do you? You push and you
push until you get exactly what you want."

"That's not true. What I want is you here with me,
every night. I want a life with you. And I've been very
careful to step back and let you take your time with
this."

"A life… with me?" Lola's mouth worked as she
tried to pull herself out of her fury. "We can barely get
through dinner. I don't think this is going to work. I'm
sorry. I… I have to go."

Lola fled into the night, grateful that Gage didn't follow. Back at the Laughing Mermaid, she snuck into her room, not wanting to speak with anyone.

Refusing to cry, she picked up her phone and made a call.

"Yes, good evening. I'd like to book a flight."

CHAPTER 34

*L*ola gave herself a mental health day that Sunday, hopping on her scooter early in the morning and disappearing to the other side of the island where there was a trail she could hike to a private beach. Turning off her phone, she spent the day reading in the shade, taking a dip in the water whenever she wanted to. It was only when she floated for a while in the water that her anxiety finally calmed and she realized what a mess she'd made of things.

In theory, she understood that Gage was a nice guy and he was doing what nice guys do – trying to help. But to have someone swoop in and neatly handle all her problems like that was just… annoying. Then when he'd dropped the bomb about wanting a life with her – well, she'd panicked.

Something glinted in the water, and Lola dove for it

without thinking. Surfacing, she gasped at what she'd found, and barely made it to the shore before coming to her knees. Shuddering, she looked toward the sea, but saw nothing other than placid waves and a lazy gull swooping in the sky. For hours, Lola stayed at the beach, unable to bring herself to the leave the water, until her skin was pruned, and her mind had worked through what she needed to do.

"I hear you, okay? I just have to do this on my terms," Lola called out.

The gull cried in response, but nothing else happened. Standing, Lola crossed the beach, sand grating between her toes, and packed her stuff. Tucking her find in her knapsack, she went back to the Laughing Mermaid and packed her bag. Picking up her phone, she texted Sam.

I have a flight out in the morning. Details later. No, I don't want to talk. Yes, I'm okay.

Wait, what? Are you coming back? Lola... helloooooo.

I need space.

There had been few times Lola and Sam had asked that of each other. But when one of them did, the other respected it. Even if they didn't like it.

Fine. I love you. Call me the instant you're ready to talk.

I promise. I love you too.

That night, she barely slept. Finally, beleaguered,

she dragged herself from bed and climbed into the swing chair, rocking gently as she sketched picture after picture, trying to put all her memories of the past couple of weeks into drawings. When the sun finally rose, she grabbed her bag and slipped from the house, grateful that she didn't run into anyone.

Lola had one stop to make on her way to the airport. She dreaded it, but wouldn't be able to respect herself if she didn't at least go and apologize to Gage – face to face. Because that's what grown-ups do, Lola reminded herself the whole way to Gage's house. She took her time parking her scooter, noting that there was another car at his house, and wondering who was there this early in the morning. The large front door was open, and Lola dawdled a moment, pretending to sniff the blooms of a frangipani tree, stalling before she went inside. Finally, knowing she couldn't put it off any longer, Lola turned and took a few steps toward the door.

And stopped dead in her tracks.

The woman she'd seen out to dinner with Gage that night was at his house. At eight in the morning. And she was currently plastered against him, her arms locked around his neck as she pulled him into a desperate kiss.

It was all Lola needed to see before she turned and ran.

"Lola!" Gage shouted, but she didn't look back.

She raced her scooter onto the main road and then down a few other dirt roads, in case Gage decided to follow her. Too shocked and numb to even feel the pain,

Lola refused to let tears come to her eyes. Instead, she focused on the one thing she had to do.

Get off this island.

At the airport, she pulled out her phone.

"Prince? Yes, I have a favor to ask."

CHAPTER 35

"Cynthia! What the hell was that?" Gage shouted, racing back inside, ripping his hands through his hair. He was torn as to whether he should chase after Lola, or fire his assistant and kick her out of his house. Finally, he decided against chasing Lola down. If he scared her while she was on the scooter, she could have an accident or get hurt. Furious, he paced his kitchen, trying to get his breathing under control.

"I'm sorry, Gage, please don't be mad at me." Cynthia did her best to look contrite.

"What the actual fuck, Cynthia? I'm serious. What you just did was… I don't even know what to think. What to say! What were you thinking?" Gage shouted, not caring when Cynthia flinched and backed away from him. Gage paced the house, not sure what to do, but convinced that his chance with Lola was now gone.

She'd come to him.

That was all he could think; all he could see was the hurt on her face as she drove out of his life on her scooter.

"Gage, I –" Cynthia began.

"No, just don't. Not yet. I swear to god, I could throttle you right now," Gage said, still pacing, his mind racing.

"Please, hear me out," Cynthia said.

Walking over to the kitchen counter, Gage pulled out a bottle of whiskey and poured a glass. He stood at the counter for a moment, seething, before he drank the glass down in one burning gulp.

"Talk," Gage ordered.

"You see... I knew how upset you were. It's why I'm here, isn't it?"

"Yes, you did know. So to pull a stunt like that...?"

"I know. I understand why you're mad, I'm sorry."

"I need your logic. Like now."

"Well, I was kind of mad at Lola. I mean, you're such a great guy, and all you were doing was trying to help her. There was no reason she should have treated you that way. Which got me thinking that maybe she doesn't really have feelings for you. Or maybe she doesn't even *know* if she has feelings for you." Cynthia paused and clenched her teeth in remorse.

"Go on," Gage ordered.

"And well, I saw her outside, you see? You couldn't see her from where you were standing, and I saw that she was hesitant to come inside. And it just came to me in a flash – if she saw us kiss and got angry, then we'd know for sure if she really had feelings for you. Don't you see? She really cares about you, Gage. All is not lost. This is a good thing," Cynthia insisted.

Gage looked at her like she'd just grown horns.

"Did it occur to you that maybe, since she has trust issues when it comes to commitments, seeing me with another woman so soon after we'd been together would only reinforce her belief that relationships are bogus?"

"Um…" Cynthia stalled.

"No, no it did not," Gage continued, so furious he could barely see straight. "And did it occur to you that since she was coming to see me, on her own, without an invitation, maybe she felt bad and wanted to talk the argument through? And that we could have worked our way around to figuring out what her feelings are without you meddling?"

"Um…" Cynthia said again, wringing her hands.

"And that now I have to go search the island for her and try to convince her that she didn't see what she thought she did?"

"Oh, Gage. I'm so sorry. I really screwed up. I thought – I don't know, I thought I'd be forcing her hand and showing her what she really felt about you. I didn't think it through – you know I can be impulsive. Please, let me go find her and explain. I'll tell her the whole story. I promise I'll make it right," Cynthia pleaded.

Gage pointed a finger at her and then to the door.

"You've done enough. Handle the charters today. Call Mark in to captain. Double pay. I won't captain today. I have to find Lola and make this right."

"I'm so sorry, Gage. You know I love you and I only have your best interests at heart." Cynthia was openly crying again.

"I understand that. And when I'm done being mad, I'll forgive you. But right now? I need you out of my face."

"I'm gone. I'll do anything you need to make up for it. I promise."

"Just go."

Gage glanced at the whiskey bottle once more after Cynthia left, but he knew he shouldn't have another. Instead, he grabbed his keys and hit the road. First, he drove past the Laughing Mermaid and Lucas and Sam's house, looking for Lola's scooter. Not finding it there, he stopped by the coconut hut to see it locked up tight. For the next hour, he drove the island, stopping at any rental scooter that looked like hers, before finally giving up and returning home. Once there, he picked up his phone and called Lucas.

"Hey, Lucas, Gage here. Long time no chat. Um, question for you – is Lola with you? Or have you seen her?"

Gage waited while Lucas passed the phone to Sam.

"Hey, Sam. Have you seen Lola? I'm looking for her."

"Gage, what's going on? Did you two have a fight?"

"Yes, kind of. Well, yes, and then a misunderstanding. I'd really like to find her and explain," Gage said, trying not to spill Lola's business, knowing she'd be mad at him if he did.

"Gage, she caught a flight out this morning. She's not talking to me right now. She asked for space. It's rare that she does that, so I had to respect it."

Gage closed his eyes and cursed, long and low.

"Do you know if she'll be back? Where she's going?"

"She didn't say. I'm so sorry, Gage. I'll keep messaging her and let you know anything I can when I have more details."

"Thanks, Sam."

"Gage?"

"Yeah?"

"Don't give up on her. She's a tough one, but she needs someone she can rely on."

"The problem is, she now thinks I'm untrustworthy."

"Shit."

"Indeed."

CHAPTER 36

*L*ola held onto the numb feeling, refusing to break, reminding herself over and over that she was strong. If Irmine could weather the devastating loss of Nalachi, the father of her children, Lola could certainly handle the pain of losing someone she'd never really had. She carried the numbness through overseeing the packing of her apartment, and got in her landlord's face until he backed down and agreed to not charge her the penalty for breaking her lease in exchange for her agreeing not to take him to court for refusing to allow the moving company to pack her things.

The numbness stayed with her on her stop to Calista Island, the neighboring island that Prince's cousin lived on. From there she had a lovely day touring workshops and sourcing furniture for Siren Moon and meeting with local artists. It was the first sliver of joy she'd felt in days, and she held onto that with the hope that the numbness would fade in time and she'd be back to her normal resilient self soon enough.

Lola had deleted all of Gage's messages – both voice and text – without reading or opening them. Sam, true to her word, gave her space, except for one text message asking if she was okay when Lola hadn't checked in after a couple of days. She did respond to that, because Sam was her family, and then finally placed a call she'd been avoiding.

"I'll be fine, Mom. This one just stung more than others."

"Tell me what happened, baby. I'm so sorry you're hurting," Miriam said, her voice surprisingly clear for the distance. Lola sat at an outdoor café across from the airport, waiting for her plane to Siren Island.

"Where are you?" Lola stalled, sipping her rum and Coke. She was grateful she'd snagged a shady spot, as there wasn't a cloud in the sky today.

"Denmark, if you can believe that," Miriam laughed, as if to say, 'Why in the world would I ever go to Denmark?'

"I can believe it. I like Denmark."

"Oh, well, so do I, but you know I much prefer southern Europe. I'm thinking Portofino next. Though I do have a friend hosting a lovely art show in Portugal in a few weeks. Maybe I'll fly there for a while. It's a lovely time of year to be there, if you remember?"

"I do, yes. Portugal is a favorite, for sure," Lola said, her tone listless.

"Okay, enough stalling. Tell me."

And so Lola did, leaving nothing out except the magick and mermaids, because – well, that was private. The rest, though, she dropped right on her mother's shoulders. By the time she was finished, her drink was gone, and her plane was getting ready to board.

"You need to talk to him," Miriam said immediately.

"I tried. He was too busy sucking face with someone else to notice."

"That's absolutely untrue."

"What? I know what I saw. How can you be so sure?"

"A man doesn't try to save you, take care of you, and solve all your problems – and then cheat on you. Those are two different kinds of men. Trust me."

"You can't possibly know that."

"Oh, I do know that. The men who cheat? They're entirely self-focused. They need attention. They want excitement, to feel like they're the biggest, baddest man in the room. The men who want to be the hero? Who want to save you? They get their rush from making sure their woman is taken care of and happy. That's the man you hold onto."

"Have you known any of these men?"

"Sure, I've been lucky to know a few in my life. And when we parted, it was of mutual accord – not because of hurt feelings and lies. Trust me on this, Lola, this man does not want to hurt you. Oh, my darling, please give him a chance. It's the one thing I've wanted for you." Miriam sniffled into the phone a bit. "To find someone who would put you first. You need love in your life. I've been so worried for you."

"Worried for me? Why? I've been fine."

"You've been drifting for quite a while now. And that's fine and dandy. But now? Your own gallery! And a man who loves you. Oh, just do me a favor and don't go all ice queen on this man. I know you're an independent woman, and nobody is trying to take that from you. But remember that when you let people help, it's doing them a favor too. How does it feel when you help people?"

"I feel good. I like to help people."

"So why wouldn't you let someone who loves you try to help? It makes them feel good."

"Because I need to know I can do this on my own," Lola said, stubborn to the end.

"Do what on your own?" Miriam asked, exasperated. "You've done everything on your own since you could toddle away from me. Isn't it time to share your light with someone else?"

"I… Mom, my plane's boarding. I love you."

"Just think about what I said. Call me soon. You know I'm always here for you."

"I know that, Mom. You're the absolute best and I love you always."

"Safe flight."

The whole ride back to Siren Island, all Lola could think about was what her mother had said.

Those two different types of men.

Maybe she'd only ever known the first.

CHAPTER 37

a knock sounded at her door.

Lola ignored it, but then heard Irma's voice through the door.

"This is an intervention. If we don't see you down at the beach in the next ten minutes, I will use this key and drag you out of there."

Lola looked at the door in shock.

"Yes, you heard me correctly. Ten minutes. Don't worry, no men allowed."

Lola sighed and stood up from where she'd nestled back into her swing chair, rocking herself over and over in a soothing motion as she tried to figure out how she wanted to handle things. Stalling, she looked in the pretty shell jewelry dish by the mirror where her necklace lay, along with her find from the other day. Taking a deep breath, she put them both on, and met her eyes in the mirror.

"You are powerful beyond your belief."

With that, Lola left the room and followed the foot-path to the beach where Irma, Jolie, Mirra, and Sam all sat around a little bonfire. They'd pulled up little bean bag chairs and were talking quietly among themselves. When Sam saw her, she stood up and launched herself at Lola.

"I hate when you don't talk to me," Sam said, "but I'm glad you're back."

"I'm sorry. I shouldn't shut you out. I'll try not to do it again," Lola said, hugging her back tightly. "I love you and I know you're always there for me, but that wasn't right of me to make you worry."

"I know you can take care of yourself. I do. But I just wanted to know you were okay," Sam said, pulling back, firelight glinting on the tears in her eyes.

"Don't cry, Sami. Please? I'm fine."

"I know…" Sam led her to a poofy chair, pushed her down to sit and handed her a drink. A strong one. Lola approved.

"Before we get into anything," Irma interrupted, and Lola looked up at her. She stood by the fire, her hands clasped behind her back. She wore a simple white sheath that dropped to her feet, her hair flowing behind her almost to her waist, and a riot of turquoise necklaces hung from her neck. She looked like a high priestess, Lola thought, and then hunched her shoulders when Irma gave her the sternest look she'd seen yet from the woman.

"You don't do that, you understand?" Irma asked.

"I…" Lola looked around at the other girls, but they all were glaring at her too – except for Sam, who was wiping tears.

"You don't just leave like that. You have family here now. It's not fair to us, those who care about you. And you've hurt Gage."

"Wait a minute –" Lola said, but Irma held up her finger to stop her.

"We'll get to Gage. I know you were hurt and that you're learning a lot about yourself. So I'll give you a pass on this one. This is your warning. You don't run away with your tail tucked between your legs and not let your friends know where you are or what's wrong. That's not how you treat people who love you."

"I… You're absolutely right," Lola realized, feeling the numbness she'd been holding onto for days crack and all the feelings come flooding through. "I'm so sorry. You're completely right. I should have spoken to you."

"You don't have to handle everything on your own. If you're hurting, we're hurting," Mirra said, her voice soft, her eyes luminous in the fire.

"I am hurting," Lola admitted. "And I was wrong to not tell you what was going on. But I think since I knew I was coming back, I figured I could explain it later."

"How could we have known you were coming back?" Jolie asked, her glare game strong tonight. "You didn't bother to tell us you were leaving. You barely even told Sam – your very best friend. She had no clue if you'd even be returning here. That's not nice. That's not what we do."

"I'm sorry, Sam."

"I know you are. And I know you, through and through. So I knew you had to go like you did. I just hope that, now that you're back, you'll be willing to let us be a family to you. You need a foundation, Lola. You've been running for years. We're here."

"Mermaids don't run away, and they don't leave their tribe behind," Irma said, piercing Lola with a look so powerful that she swore her heart skipped a beat.

"Excuse me?" Lola whispered.

"You heard exactly what I said. Mermaids are strong and vulnerable at the same time. And we never leave our tribe behind."

"What are you saying to me, exactly?" Lola didn't want to blurt out her suspicions and she looked wildly around the circle until her eyes landed on a beaming Sam. "Is this real?"

Sam nodded, tears in her eyes. "They're mermaids."

"And so are you," Irma said to Lola.

Lola looked at her like she'd grown two heads. "Um, pretty sure I'm not." Lola laughed out loud, then just looked around as they all stared at her in silence.

"The necklace you wear?"

"Yes?" Lola looked down at where the shell locket nestled at her chest, humming its happy little hum by her heart.

"Open it and look in the mirror."

Lola looked at Irma and then down at the locket, before reaching down and opening it up. Shocked, she almost dropped the mirror, then held it closer to her face, twisting to get the light of the fire.

It was her… but not her. Her eyes glowed fiercely green in her face, and her hair seemed redder somehow, coiling in thick ropes around her head, and her skin glowed as if lit from within by the moon.

"I… what's happening?" Lola looked down at her drink, then over at Sam.

"It's true, Lola. Mermaids are real," Sam said, happy to finally share her secret.

"I know that," Lola said automatically. "I realized it pretty much the first day I got here. I could feel it in my soul. But I thought it would be best not to say anything. I want to respect people's privacy. It's… I just can't wrap my head around what a magnificent discovery this is. I'm honored to know you all. Thank you for sharing this with me."

"But don't you see?" Sam said softly. "What they're trying to tell you is that there is a *reason* why you were drawn here. Why you've put down roots here, for the first time ever. Why you've felt so listless and untethered."

"Sam, seriously, how would I not know I was mermaid?"

"You have some of it, in your blood. Not full mermaid," Irma interrupted. "But you were gifted the necklace, and it gives you the power to change, if you will it."

"Shut. Up," Lola exclaimed.

"I most certainly will not," Irma said, but smiled at her.

"So, to be clear, you're saying if I walk on down to the water, with this necklace on, and just will it – I'll change into a mermaid? As I will it, so mote it be? And all that? You guys are pulling my leg," Lola laughed.

Nobody else laughed.

"Is this like – okay, you're punking me for leaving the island like I did. You just want me jump into the ocean at night and get all wet?"

"Lola, you know it's true. You've received many other gifts since you've arrived. Both in experiences, and in actual gifts. You wear another now. It's not for you, though. What will you do with it?"

Lola looked down at what she had found the other day.

"I need to give it to Gage," she said, softly.

"You know what it means," Irma said.

"I do."

"Then what are you waiting for?"

"Um, I guess I can drive up there and see if he's home. I need to talk this out with him before I even go through it all with you. Is it okay if I leave you?" Lola asked, suddenly desperate to see Gage and make things right.

. . .

"YES, GO GET YOUR MAN!" Sam crowed.

"Okay." Lola stood and turned.

"Not that way." Irma stopped her and pointed at the ocean.

"Wait… you want me to swim to his house?"

"Trust," Irma said, tapping Lola's necklace.

"Well, shit," Lola said, and then looked at the other girls, who all nodded.

"You'll be safe. We promise you," Mirra said softly. "Our tribe looks out for each other."

"He needs you, Lola," Jolie agreed.

"Does he know… about mermaids?" Sam asked, her eyes on Lola.

"He believes," Lola said.

"Show yourself to him," Irma insisted. "Now, go. The hour grows late."

With one last glance at the women standing by the fire, Lola walked to the shoreline. Then, pulling her dress over her head and tossing it on the beach, she dove into darkness.

CHAPTER 38

*L*ola kicked below the surface and, remembering what Irma said, she touched her necklace and willed herself to change.

And she did.

Lola almost choked on water in shock – one moment she was kicking with two legs and the next she was zipping through the water, seeming not to need air, and able to see just fine even though it was night. It was unlike anything she'd ever known, and for a moment she thought she never wanted to come out. Zipping to the surface – and how she even knew where the surface was in the darkness, Lola didn't know – she popped out of the water.

"Woohoo!" Lola shouted, unable to hide her joy, and the women on the beach cheered. Pipin raced to the water's edge and barked at her.

.   .   .

"EMBRACE YOUR POWER!" Jolie called.

"On it," Lola shouted, and dipped back under the water, unable to resist the way it felt to flow through the water as if she weighed nothing at all. For just a moment, she allowed herself to bask in the beauty that was the sheer magick of the universe. Then she swam on, knowing instinctively when to surface.

She could see Gage, sitting alone on his deck, his head in his hands. Her heart hurt for him, knowing she had caused a good man pain, and she swam closer. For a moment, she hoped to slip from the water and change before he saw her, but then she remembered Irma's instructions.

Show yourself to him.

In for a penny, in for a pound, Lola thought, and taking a deep breath, she called to him.

"Gage."

Gage whipped his head up and looked around in confusion, standing up on his deck.

"Gage, here, in the water."

Gage bent and peered over the railing. Pipin barked from where he had followed Lola down the shoreline, making sure she was safe.

"Lola? Are you swimming? Is that Pipin? What the hell are you doing in the water at night? Don't move, I'm coming down," Gage shouted, and she could see him race through the house. When he came to the beach, he had towels in his hands, and her heart melted a little more. This was a man she had hurt, and still he brought towels down for her.

Gage stopped at the waterline, putting the towels down on the sand, and just looked at where her head and shoulders popped out of the water.

"Lola, what are you doing?" Gage asked.

"I'm sorry I left," Lola said.

"That's okay, we'll work through it. Just… can you get out of the water? I need to see you. I have to explain what happened –"

"Gage, I understand. We'll talk, but first… I have to show you something," Lola said, her voice almost a whisper as she worried what he would think.

"Show me what? Lola, are you okay? You look a little…" Gage's voice trailed off.

"Gage, this is me," Lola said, and flipped her tail out of the water. The moon flashed off her beautiful scales, and Lola almost laughed at the sheer enchantment of it all.

Gage stood, stunned, his mouth hanging open.

"Gage?" Lola asked softly.

"My wish came true," he whispered.

"It really did," Lola laughed, ecstatic in her newfound power.

"I wished for my own mermaid. I wanted to believe in them so much. Just for once in my life, to have some-thing fanciful and full of magick. I wanted to believe so badly, and I thought I'd found that with you and then I worried I screwed it up… and here you are. Oh my god, a real live mermaid! Did you know? Is this what you were keeping from me? I have to touch you," Gage said and strode right into the water until he was next to her.

"Can I?" Gage asked, his eyes hot in the moonlight.

"You can," Lola said, and laughed into his mouth when he pulled her to him, kissing her. He tasted of salt and tears, and Lola never wanted to let him go.

"This is incredible. Lola, you take my breath away."

"I just found out tonight, so I'm pretty new to all this," Lola admitted, flapping her tail about and giggling a bit. "But I'd like to change and come inside. Is that okay? I want to talk to you. We need to work this out. I don't want to run anymore, Gage."

"Good, because I won't let you run anymore."

"I'm... going to change now?" Lola laughed. "I don't really know how it all works, but I guess I just have to will it. Give me a second." Lola dove beneath the surface and on her command, she was back to her normal legs.

This was trippy, was all she could think. Then she surfaced again and walked with him to the shoreline, his eyes huge.

"Oh god, you're beautiful," Gage whispered, and Lola realized she was completely naked. "But you look cold, let me wrap you up." Gage bent and grabbed towels, running over to wrap them around her.

Miriam was right, Lola thought; this was not a man who would cheat.

"Will you come upstairs with me?" Gage asked.

"I'd love nothing more," Lola said, and he swept her into his arms, pressing kisses down her neck. Finally he deposited her on the bed, and pulled out a robe to wrap her in. Once he'd tended to her, he kneeled at her feet.

"Lola, you have to know this – I did not cheat on you. Cynthia – well, in her harebrained way, she was trying to help. She wanted to prove to you that you had feelings for me. It was misguided and wrong, but I didn't know she was going to do it. If you remember at all, I wasn't even touching her, I was so shocked."

Lola thought back to the moment and realized he was right. It was Cynthia plastered against Gage; his arms had been at his sides.

"Thank you for the explanation. I understand you're a good man. I came over to apologize to you, actually," Lola said, and then ran her hands through Gage's hair when he buried his face at her knees. "I need to learn to be better about accepting help. And realizing that allowing a partner into my life doesn't invalidate me or make me weaker, because our shared love only makes us stronger."

Gage looked up, hope in his eyes.

"I have something for you," Lola whispered. Reaching up, she pulled a chain from her neck.

"Is this my necklace? Wait… no, is it?" Gage said and stared at the pendant in his hand. It was his pendant, but it had been changed since its time in the cave. Instead of the simple pendant with the stars and the moon on it, the ring she had offered in the wishing cave had been melded around it, forming a braided gold border, and two tiny seed pearls had been embedded on the star and the moon.

"It's been changed. For us. It's a gift."

"Our souls together," Gage said automatically, recognizing the meaning of the pearls.

"Mine for yours. My gift to you, Gage. My promise to be your partner in this life and the next."

PIPIN RACED back down the shoreline, finding the women by the fire once more, barking in excitement.

Irma bent down and nuzzled him, before looking up at the ladies around the fire.

"And all is as it should be."

*M*usic played from an impromptu band that had just shown up, and Lola smiled, leaning into Gage for a moment as she looked around at what she had created. It was Siren Moon's grand opening party, and it felt like the entire island had turned out for the occasion.

"You should be proud of yourself," Gage said. "I know I am. Just look at how magickal this is. You did this, Lola."

"I really did, didn't I? With your help and the help of others, of course," Lola said, turning to press a kiss against his lips before looking back at her happy little gallery.

Fairy lights were strung among the palms and all through the back garden, where a food and drinks table had been set up in front of her brand-new studio. The tables and chairs she'd brought in were full, but nobody seemed to mind – some people perched on walls; others had brought their own chairs. The inside of Siren Moon was outfitted for her first show, all based around a theme that seemed just right for the occasion.

Believe.

"You've got yourself your first sale." Miss Maureen sauntered over, looking resplendent in a deep green dress splashed with yellow flowers. "I want that black and white photo – the one where you can just think you're glimpsing a mermaid under the water. It's mine and you can't sell it to nobody else."

"It is yours, but it's a gift."

"No, I want to be your first sale." Miss Maureen put her hands at her waist and set in to argue.

"I refuse. Remember I told you that I had a print for you? In exchange for my gorgeous mermaid dress?" Lola wore it tonight, and had received so many compliments on it that Miss Maureen might have to close her bookshop and take up crocheting full-time.

"I suppose I do."

"That's the print. It's meant for you."

"Now isn't that just the sweetest! But how am I going to be your first sale then?"

"Find something else to buy." Lola laughed when Miss Maureen swatted her and then hustled back into the store, shooing someone away from a necklace that Jolie had crafted. Prince danced by with his granddaughter, shooting Lola a cheeky grin.

"This here's just what I wanted for the space, pretty

lady."

"Thank you for everything, Prince. You're my hero," Lola called as he danced away, laughing all the while.

"Hey, now, I can't have you flirting with other men," Gage pouted, and Lola leaned into him again.

"You're also my hero."

"I hope so, because I have a surprise for you," Gage said, checking his watch and then turning as a car pulled up.

"What is it?" Lola narrowed her eyes, suspicious of surprises.

"One moment," Gage said, and went to the car, pulling the door open and turning to see Lola's face when Miriam stepped out. She looked as coolly lovely as she always did, in a brilliant red dress with a funky orange and white necklace twisted around her throat.

"Mom!" Lola gasped, and ran to Miriam, her heart in her throat.

"Well, now, I couldn't miss your big opening, could I?"

"I'm so glad you're here. Everyone I love is here," Lola said. There were tears in her eyes as she looked back at what she'd created, and smiled to see all her favorite people in one spot.

"It's absolutely perfect," Miriam said, kissing her cheek. "You've created your home."

And in that moment, Lola realized – this was what she'd been searching for all along.

AFTERWORD

**A Good Chance: Book 3 in the Siren Island Series –
Available now!**

https://www.triciaomalley.com/the-siren-island-series

To sign up for notifications of a new release, fun giveaways and special offers please go to
http://eepurl.com/1LAiz

Please consider leaving a review! A book can live or die
by the reviews alone. It means a lot to an author to
receive reviews and I greatly appreciate it!

Living in the Caribbean has helped to inspire my
descriptions of Siren Island. If it wasn't for my love of
the ocean, and the mysteries that lie within, I would

never have been able to write these books. Thank you for coming along on my journey.

A special thanks to Jayne Rylon and Lila Dubois for keeping me on track when writing this book. You ladies are amazing!

As always, you can reach me at
info@triciaomalley.com
or feel free to visit my website at
www.triciaomalley.com.

You can also find me on Facebook by searching Tricia O'Malley or using this link.

https://www.facebook.com/Tricia-OMalley-283571038502937/

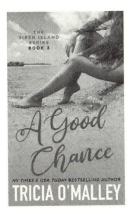

Continue the Siren Island Series now- Available now as an e-book or paperback.

Sign up for information on new releases, free books, and fun giveaways at my website www.triciaomalley.com

The following is an excerpt from A Good Chance

Book 3 in the Siren Island Series. Available on all e-book stores.

https://www.triciaomalley.com/the-siren-island-series

CHAPTER 1

"*I*'m sorry, but – you did what?"

"I signed up for a reality show on an island in the Caribbean. Well, like a competition, actually."

"And why would you – or anyone – *do* such a thing?" Avery pushed her glasses up on her face and pinched the bridge of her nose, a dull ache beginning to pound in her head. It was inevitable, because her twin sister Ruby came with a side of headaches, Avery thought, and eyed her sister warily. She might as well have been looking in a mirror, aside from the fact that Ruby had recently added blond highlights to her auburn hair and sported a small beauty mark above her lip. Otherwise, they were identical twins, both strong, lean, and with a massive head of riotous curls that had encouraged more than one man to make lewd comments about the red-headed sisters.

"Oh, come on," Ruby pouted, pushing her thick lower lip out and bracing her hands on her hips. "Where's your sense of adventure?"

"Right where it should be – with reasonable things like ziplining in Costa Rica or discovering a new restaurant in Times Square."

"Like you would *ever* zipline in Costa Rica." Ruby rolled her eyes and crossed the bedroom to start rummaging through Avery's closet, a habit that was long ingrained but had never ceased to put Avery on edge. It wasn't that she minded sharing her clothes; it was that Ruby pulled them all out of order and staunchly refused to put them away, leaving a heap of discarded dresses and shirts on Avery's pink tufted velvet chair, her one concession to whimsy in her bedroom.

"I might. You don't know that. And if I do, it's not going to be with a bunch of cameras trained on me so my terror can be publicized to the whole world."

"The winner gets $100,000," Ruby said, pulling a brilliant green shirtdress, spotted with white lilies, from the closet and holding it in front of her. Avery hadn't even worn it yet, but she was so shocked by Ruby's comment that she ignored Ruby when she tossed the dress over her tote bag.

"Are you kidding me? For going to a Caribbean island? Is this even a real show? That's an insane amount of money." Avery mentally calculated all the bills she could pay off – from student loans to her outstanding medical bills from a traumatic accident a few years ago.

"See? Not sounding so stupid now, is it?"

"But what do you know about this show? How did you even get on it? How do you win money? Do you really have to be on television?" Avery peppered her sister with questions, pushing her notebook aside and giving Ruby her full attention. Ruby flopped onto the bed, crossing legs clad in screaming yellow skinny jeans, and flipped her hair over her shoulder.

"The island is called Siren Island, and from what I've read they have a lot of mermaid myths on the island. How cool is that?" Ruby asked, avoiding the questions. Avery was well-versed with Ruby's tactics, and just stared her down.

"Okay, fine, it's called *Swept Away,* and I applied for it months and months ago. I actually totally forgot until, like, a month or so ago, when they called me in for casting and I went through more rounds of interviews. Then I signed all the contracts and it's set to start soon. You win money if you and the bachelor choose each other, and you have to make it through certain challenges. It's kind of like a dating game and an island survival game in one."

"Island survival game." Avery immediately pictured spiders and cockroaches crawling over her legs in a sandy tent.

"Yup. But like... posh, you know?" Ruby tilted her head and gave Avery a blinding smile, which immediately set off all of Avery's internal warning signs. Ruby was about to ask Avery to do something for her. A very big something.

It had been like this their whole lives, Avery thought. She'd followed her dazzling sister through a series of adventures as they grew up. Well, more like she'd tried to stop Ruby from being so reckless, and had always been her clean-up crew and moral support when things went up in flames. Ruby was impulsive, and dove head-first into any fleeting whim she had, while Avery made lists of pros and cons and consulted others for advice before making a big decision. It suited her well as an engineer, but was often cause for arguments between the sisters. Mainly, Ruby arguing that Avery needed to lighten up a bit.

The last time she'd taken that advice, however, she'd gone kayaking with her then-boyfriend, Mr. Outdoors Colorado Man, who had inadvertently taken her down a Class V rapids. Avery had been rewarded with several broken bones, a month-long stay at the hospital, a week in a medically-induced coma, more medical bills than she cared to think about, and a now ex-boyfriend. If she'd just followed her gut and taken the less risky approach, she'd have enjoyed having a picnic by the river and watching the birds fly by above. Instead, with Ruby's words in the back of her head, she'd broken out of her comfort zone – and had broken her body in doing so.

"What do you want?" Avery said, reaching back to massage the tightness from her neck.

"Well, you see, when I signed up for the show, I hadn't met Zane yet." Ruby pouted once more, and Avery almost rolled her eyes. Zane was Ruby's latest fling, an Australian surf instructor. She'd heard all the details about him, including his infamous moves in the bedroom, for two months now.

"Right, and he probably won't like you going on a show to hook up with some dude," Avery said, shrugging a shoulder. "Simple. Don't go on the show."

"Erm... not that simple," Ruby said, smiling that bright smile at Avery again. "They've already got my picture up, social media profile, website...all the stuff. And I signed contracts."

"So? Go on the show then. I'm sure Zane will understand. He seems pretty adventurous."

"Yeah... about that." Ruby bit down on her lip again and Avery wanted to scream.

"Just say it. I know you're easing me into it, but I swear to god, Ruby, I've told you a million times – it's easier to just rip the Band-Aid off. What do you need?"

"See... that's the other part. Zane and I just bought a world ticket."

Avery just looked at her sister blankly.

"A..."

"A world ticket. It's this open-ended plane ticket where you can travel the world in one direction and hit a bunch of countries so long as you use it in six months."

"Okay, and? So go after the show."

"I leave next week," Ruby said, the look on her face both sheepish and excited.

"Wait… what? You're leaving next week to travel the entire world? For months and months? And you're just telling me now?" Avery shrieked, "What about rent? What about our apartment? What about your houseplants?"

"You pay most of the rent, because I'm never here," Ruby pointed out. "And I always kill the houseplants anyway."

"What about your job?"

"I can always pick up another marketing gig, Avery, it's fine." Ruby shrugged.

"But… what about me? You're just going to leave me?" Avery asked, her eyes round in her face. Despite their differences, the sisters had an unbreakable bond and as much as Ruby annoyed Avery, she'd still miss the hell out of her sister.

"I'll be back. It's okay – this is good for you, Avery. You need to break out of your comfort zone. I'm worried for you… ever since you got hurt –" Ruby's eyes filled at the mere mention of the accident – "you've gone all hermitville on me. You were bad before, but now it's just work, gym, and watching Netflix. You need to be out, experiencing life. You're twenty-seven, not retired. You need to break out of this rut."

"I'm not traveling the world with you, Ruby. I have

a job. One that I quite like, actually," Avery said, pushing aside Ruby's comments about her being a hermit.

"I didn't ask you to travel the world with me. Even I know I can't get you that far out of your comfort zone. But you are owed a vacation. You haven't taken one since you started at the firm three years ago," Ruby said, raising an eyebrow at Avery.

"So? I'll take one. Soon. I promise."

"Great! I'm glad you said that, because I need you to take my place on the show," Ruby said, smiling her con-artist smile at her sister. Avery, for once, was left without words, and she stared at her sister with a mixture of panic and anger.

"No. Nope. No way. Never, *ever*, happening," Avery finally said when she could breathe again. "A love show? On an island?" She might as well have said – Smoking crack? With a side of acid?

"You have to, Avery. They can sue me if I don't go on. The contract says so."

"What kind of contract did you sign, Ruby? That sounds like slave labor. Tell them you're sick. That's life. I'm *so* not doing this."

"Please? Just think, you'll be a perfect shoe-in for me. And you could win $100,000. That's enough to pay off all those bills and put you in the clear for your future."

"I think you and I both know the likelihood of me

winning an adventure challenge – and a man's heart – on a game show are slim to none."

"You'd be surprised. It's always the unexpected one who wins."

"No, Ruby. A hard no."

"Just think about it. All that money. A vacation in the sun. Cute guys…" Ruby smiled at her.

"Not happening."

"But you never take risks anymore. Is this what you want from your life?"

Avery's mouth dropped open. She was about to protest when she realized Ruby was right. She'd been cautious even before the accident, but after? It had spun her into a life of taking very few chances. Unless, of course, Ruby dragged her into something.

But either way, a reality show was not happening. Going out of her comfort zone was more along the lines of trying online dating or eating at a new fusion restaurant. Going on television? So. Not. Happening.

Continue reading Book 3 in the Siren Island Series. Available on all e-book stores.
https://www.triciaomalley.com/the-siren-island-series

THE ISLE OF DESTINY SERIES

ALSO BY TRICIA O'MALLEY

Stone Song

Sword Song

Spear Song

Sphere Song

Available as an e-book, paperback or audiobook!

https://www.triciaomalley.com/home-3

"Love this series. I will read this multiple times. Keeps you on the edge of your seat. It has action, excitement and romance all in one series."

-Amazon Review-

"I have read thousands of books and a fair percentage have been romances. Until I read Wild Irish Heart, I never had a book actually make me believe in love."

-Amazon Review-

THE STOLEN DOG

ALSO BY TRICIA O'MALLEY

A non-fiction account of our dog being stolen and how we recovered him. A read that will renew your faith in humanity. All proceeds donated to animal rescues. For a list of organizations you have helped by buying one of Tricia O'Malley's books here is the link to a blog post thanking her readers.

Available as an e-book or paperback!

https://bit.ly/2IRQKbM

ACKNOWLEDGMENTS

First, and foremost, my friends for their constant support, advice, and ideas. You've all proven to make a difference on my path. And, to my beta readers, I love you for all of your support and fascinating feedback!

And last, but never least, my two constant companions as I struggle through words on my computer each day - Briggs and Blue.

As always, you can reach me at
info@triciaomalley.com
or feel free to visit my website at
www.triciaomalley.com.